Ann Dee Ellis

this is what I did:

Andersen Press • London

First published in Great Britain in 2007
by Andersen Press Limited
20 Vauxhall Bridge Road
London SW1V 2SA
www.andersenpress.co.uk
www.anndeeellis.com

Published in the USA by Little, Brown and Company,
a member of Hachette Book Group USA

British Library Cataloguing in Publication Data available

ISBN 978 184 270 677 0

Typeset by FiSH Books, Enfield, Middx.
Printed and bound in Great Britain by
Cox & Wyman Ltd, Reading, Berkshire

To Cameron
Here's why: why not

This is What I Did:

Last week Bruce kicked me in the balls and all his buddies were there laughing and I started crying.

I was lying there crying.

Them: Wah Wah Wah Wah Wah Wah

They were chanting it and yelling it.

I didn't care.

I didn't.

After what had happened with Zyler and his dad and the whole thing, I could take anything.

I proved that at the Klondike Derby.

So I just lay there curled up and crying still.

That was Wednesday after Scouts – my first time back because Dr. Benson said I should go and my parents agreed.

When I came home I tried not to tell Dad.

I didn't want to say: Dad, I got kicked in the balls at Scouts and then they all made a circle around me.

Bruce: Watch the crapstock bawl, guys.

All of them: Wah Wah Wah Wah Wah!

So I went straight to my room. I was late because I was supposed to walk straight home from the church after Scouts.

And I did walk home, but not until they had all left and I was still -lying there on the gym floor.

Me: I'm fine, Dad.

That's what I said because since I was late; he was knocking on my door.

Me: I'm fine, Dad.

But he wouldn't let it go. He never lets it go.

Me: Okay, you can come in.

Dad: What's wrong, Logan?

He was trying not to look all worried. I could tell.

Me: Nothing's wrong.

Nothing's wrong.

He sat on my bed and I was sitting on the floor going through my comic books – just like normal. Nothing's wrong.

Dad: Tell me. Was it those boys again? Tell me right now. Was it Jack?

Me: There's nothing nothing WRONG WRONG WRONG, DAD!

It came out a lot louder than I thought it would, but not as loud as it was in my head.

I never knew what to say or how to control anything anymore.

I didn't want him to know.

Dad: You can tell me anything?.?.?.?anything. I won't get mad or try to fix it: I promise.

And he says how we can't let things go as long as we did before.

Dad: Logan, you have to tell me. You have to.

Me: I know Dad, I know. I will. If anything is wrong, I'll tell you. I'm fine.

A year ago I was fine. That's when there was nothing wrong.

A year ago, in seventh grade, I was fine.

We were living on Mulholland with the hills and the lake and the freeway and the Minute Man Gas Stop and my best friend, Zyler, ate Twinkies and Coke and hated girls, except one.

I couldn't eat Twinkies or Coke because of Mom, but I hated girls too, except one.

At school we weren't so cool but we weren't so not cool.

Zyler and I would sit and talk about whatever we wanted: aerody-namics, space-time continuum, Cami Wakefield, fencing, the Denver Nuggets, Lamborghinis, and soggy Tater Tots for darts in the school lunchroom.

No one cared what we said and we didn't care what anyone else said.

*

Now we don't live on Mulholland.

We live on Judge.

And Judge looks sort of like Mulholland: the same zip code, the same trees, the same houses with grass, the same cars and minivans.

But Judge isn't Mulholland.

When my parents were looking for a new house, a new place to go, I started checking out books.

Zyler was gone and they didn't make me go to school, so I went to the library and checked out books.

And I would just read.

Stay in my room and read.

And not talk.

And not do anything.

I didn't want to do anything.

Not talk.

I just read.

*

I have a family that is good.

There are three kids and my mom is pregnant even though she hasn't had a kid for eleven years.

When Bruce found out he said my mom and dad are sex fiends and the worst kind of sex fiends because they are old sex fiends, and then I must be a sex fiend too.

Ha, ha.

We were in the hall and there were so many people.

Everyone stopped when Bruce said the sex fiend thing. I mean, not everyone... but a lot of people stopped to see what I would say or what I would do.

I didn't know what to say or what to do.

Bruce: So, are your parents going at it twenty-four seven or is it more like twenty-three seven?

Me: Huh?

Judge isn't 100 100 100 percent all bad.

At least on Judge I have the only bedroom in the basement.

That means that I don't have to be by Mom and Dad's room.

It's not that I think they are like what Bruce said about sex and everything.

They are just normal parents.

But

I never really thought about it.

They do have three kids and Mom is old and pregnant.

They do get these weird laughing voices on sometimes even at the dinner table when they tease each other, and I used to not notice but now it makes me sick.

I like to be in the basement far away from everyone and that's it.

Sometimes I have to be in charge because Mom and Dad go on dates a lot.

I never really thought about dates before with parents.

Like, is that normal or is that not normal?

One time after we moved, Mack, one of my twin brothers, said I shouldn't be in charge.

I was eating a sandwich at the table and Mack and Ryan were sitting on the couch eating chips.

Mack: Just because he's the oldest doesn't mean he should be in charge.

Mom: I'm not talking about this right now.

Mack: Mom, he's such a loser. He ruins everything.

Ryan laughed.

Mom stopped washing the dishes and looked at him and then at me and then back at him. Mom in a talk-shout: Don't you ever, ever say something like that about your brother. Ever!

She slammed the plate she was holding on the counter, walked over to the couch, yanked Mack up, and took him into the office.

Ryan laughed again.

I took another bite of sandwich.

They were in the office for a long time.

The twins are eleven and I'm thirteen and it's true: Just because I'm oldest doesn't mean I should be in charge.

Mack didn't want to move to Judge even though it didn't really matter. He and Ryan do whatever they want anyway and they're always together. Plus, they found out there's a full basketball court at the park at the end of our street and plus, Mom drives them back to Mulholland for school because it is not far and because of basketball. Mack just likes to complain and he gets upset about everything.

For a while "being in charge" wasn't an issue because Mom and Dad didn't really go out or do anything after the Zyler thing.

But then: Back to normal. Everything needs to get back to normal, Dad said.

And plus, I was fine. Just fine.

Dad works at Core Rotating. He's worked there for years and he makes rotators for signs.

That means the turning McDonald's sign and the turning piano on top of Jorgensen's Music have machines under them that have rotators that make them turn because of torque.

He even helped with the biggest one ever made, at NASCAR. It holds a car and a gigantic sign.

In school I thought it might help.

Me: My dad helped make the rotator for the biggest sign in the country, at the NASCAR racetrack.

Mr. Lopez: That's very interesting, Logan. Isn't that interesting, class?

No one said anything or looked up even. Except a girl I found out was named Laurel, and she smiled.

When I sat down I heard this: Hey, rotator retard?.?.?.?why don't you rotate your ass out of here?

It was hissed so that Mr. Lopez couldn't hear. I didn't look back to see who it was because that was the first day at Alta Jr. High. I couldn't look back.

I think it was Luke Randall who said it.

That was back in first term of this year – eighth grade – and I never knew for sure because Luke and Bruce and Toby were all in that class.

But Luke was the closest to my seat.

They all laughed though.

Even the girls like Carmen and Vanessa and Mallory.

But then one thing happened: The girl I found out was named Laurel handed me a piece of paper after class and then disappeared sort of.

The paper said this:

NASCAR = RACECAR
RACECAR = PALINDROME

Encarta Online Dictionary: Palindrome 1. text reading the same backward as forward: a word, phrase, passage, or number that reads the same forward and backward, e.g. "Anna," "Draw, o coward."

And I guess, racecar.

Racecar racecar.

Laurel is in two of my classes this term.

She has a big nose.

I like it.

*

9

For the first few weeks of school I rode the bus instead of walked, like Zyler and I used to do. Because Judge was too far away from Alta Jr. High and maybe I'd make some friends.

That was Mom's idea because she tried to have friends everywhere.

Even on Judge before we moved there because she had found out phone numbers of the neighbors and introduced herself.

Hi, I'm Silvia Paloney and my family and I are going to be moving into the Carter house.

Pause

Yes, we're really excited.

Pause

Uh-huh.

Pause

Well it's great to meet you, Lucille. We're really excited to move into the neighborhood.

Pause

Uh, well, actually we don't live too far away. We're just on the west side by the lake, but we wanted to move into a new environment – get away from the freeway.

Pause

Uh-huh.

Pause

Umm, yeah, my husband works at a place downtown so we didn't want to move too far away but, you know, just to a better situation.

Pause

Well, it's sort of hard to explain. The easiest way to put it is we need a change – Especially my oldest boy.

And then she would start to whisper because she knew I was on the computer, seven point two steps away.

It was almost the same conversation with everyone: the Smiths, the Knights, the Hongs, the Taylors, the Andersons.

And it didn't matter except it meant that before we even got to Judge my mom had friends: friends who knew she had a reject son for a son.

Mom and Dad met in HIGH SCHOOL.

They were both, I think, the popular ones in high school because you can feel it in the way they talk about it and how they want me to be excited about school and everything.

Plus how they looked.

Dad was hunky with muscles and football arms, says Mom.

Mom had long hair that was straight and, my dad says, super sexy.

Plus, he said she had a very swayey walk that she still uses, he says.

But first he dated one of my mom's best friends.

Mom: He was going out with my best friend?.?.?.? but not my very best friend, just one of my best friends.

Dad: Your mother had a lot of best friends and I had to make my way through all of them to get to her.

Ha ha kiss kiss sex fiends?

I think I might be sort of messed up.

I used to have only one best friend and it was Zyler. And nobody ever dated him or me or anybody.

But there was Cami Wakefield.

She didn't live on Mulholland.

She lived on Oak and that was three streets down from Zyler and four houses in past the fire hydrant, and her house was the one with the blue shutters and the bushes that were trimmed into pinwheels.

They weren't really pinwheels – they were more like spirals.

And Mr. Wakefield was always out clipping the bushes when we rode by on our bikes. But we never stopped.

We'd just ride by and act like it was normal and we would do this: see if maybe Cami was helping her dad or maybe pulling weeds or something.

I remember the last time we did it.

It was the afternoon before that night.

Everything was the same except now that I think about it, nothing was the same.

Cami's dad wasn't outside and Cami wasn't outside.

And I just rode really fast like I always did in case someone saw me.

But Zyler didn't.

He was sort of riding slower than usual.

I should have guessed then.

I should have known something was going to happen.

Why did it have to happen, Zyler?

I figured out some more palindromes like racecar: Mom and Dad.

Those are easy ones and dumb, but I'm going to find a cool one online or something and tell Laurel.

Maybe in a note too.

When we first moved in, this guy Jack and his wife, Patsy, came over to give us cookies and meet us.

Patsy and Mom had already chatted on the phone a couple of times and Mom thought she was really nice and probably knew

13

a lot of people.

My mom was always talking, talking so I knew Patsy knew about me.

Patsy: You must be Logan.

Me:

Patsy: Well, I've got a son your exact age. His name is Bruce.

Me:

Patsy: You are just going to love him. He's a doll.

Me:

Patsy: Are you okay?

Me: Yeah.

Mom: He's just a little shy.

Patsy: Of course. Well, Brucey is out terrorizing the neighborhood but I'll send him and his friends over to meet you first chance I get.

Me: Okay.

Patsy: It'll be good to have friends before you start a new school next week.

Me:

Mom: Thank you so much, Patsy. Logan would love it. Wouldn't you?

Me: Sure.

That same time was when Jack and my dad found out they're both mechanical engineers and they both play NBA Live on Gamecube.

And so they got to be good friends.

It used to be they would play every Sunday afternoon with other guys in the neighborhood and sometimes I would go watch.

I would go because Dad wanted me to go.

Dad: Come on, you like Gamecube. And this is a bunch of men be-ing men.

I guess I liked Gamecube all right. But there were better games on better systems and plus I didn't like to play basketball and baseball and hockey and those kinds of games.

But my dad said: Please? Come on.

I knew he wanted me to be Normal.

He wanted me to like sports like he liked sports and Mack and Ryan like sports.

So I went.

A few times.

Dad wanted me to do Scouts because he did Scouts and it was good for him.

Dad said: Logan, I promise you'll like it.

Me: I don't think so, Dad.

Dad: Please, Logan. You can trust me on this one.

Me: Why don't you make the twins do it?

Dad: They're too busy with sports. Come on, Logan. You'll love it.

He sounded weird. Desperate.

Me: I don't know.

Dad: Let's just give it a try.

So I gave it a try. I knew that there would be Bruce and Toby and Luke there, but I also knew that in Scouts you had to do a lot of stuff.

Like earn merit badges and go on campouts, which could be good and bad.

Good because maybe those guys would be distracted and not have time to harass me.

Good because maybe I would get to learn how to swim better and hike better and climb and things like that.

Good because Dad really wanted me to do it and I really wanted to do it for him too sort of.

Bad because a campout meant more time for Bruce and Toby and Luke to do stuff to me or say stuff to me or do whatever they wanted.

Bad because I knew I wasn't good at swimming and hiking and climbing and stuff like that.

Bad because if I couldn't do it or didn't want to do it, Dad would think I was a loser again.

The Scout Master was Bruce's dad, Jack.

And Dad was so glad to say that I said I would do it.

One time after NBA Live:

Jack: It'll be good for him.

Dad: Yeah, I know. And he's excited, aren't you, Logan?

Me: Yeah. Yeah.

Dad always thinks he can fix everything.

He can't.

Mack and Ryan won a basketball tournament and they got co-MVPs.

Dad says it's great and so does Mom.

They were shouting all night and yelling and high-fiving and I went in my room and it was okay.

I mean it was okay because they were good.

Zyler and I used to sort of play with Mack and Ryan sometimes.

I was so bad, they said, but Zyler had a nice shot and they liked to play with him.

We played horse and stuff and it would be funny because we'd shoot it off the roof or we'd shoot standing on the rail the twins got for their Rollerblades.

I don't play with them anymore. Even if they ask.

They were upstairs yelling and I was in my room reading about fighter jets that could almost get out of the atmosphere.

So high they were almost gone.

Gone.

*

A few months ago somebody threw a bagel with a pickle in the middle at our front door.

Mom: This has gotten out of hand.

Dad: Silvia, it's no big deal. Kids will be kids.

Mom: Tom, are you blind? Are you dumb? Are you out of your ever-loving mind? This is abuse.

Dad: Calm down.

Mom: Don't you dare tell me to calm down. Don't you dare.

Dad: Silvia?.?.?.

Mom: Tom, I've had it. I've had it. You go to work all day. You don't know. You don't see.

Dad: You think I don't see? You think I don't know? He's holed up in his room every night. And what about Jack and the whole Scout ordeal?

Mom:

Dad: And a lot of this is your fault.

Mom: What are you talking about?

Dad: Why did you tell people in the neighborhood Logan was having a hard time? You always do this. You always do this.

Mom: Oh come on, Jack. Don't blame this one on me. I'm not taking this one. I thought we agreed we wanted to protect him. I thought we agreed that we would do whatever we could.

Dad: Calling people and telling them Logan had had problems and was severely depressed did not help him, Silvia.

*

Dad bought tickets to the NBA playoffs after the Zyler thing.

Dad never buys things like playoff tickets.

And he only got two because the prices went up and we had just moved.

Dad said the tickets were for me and him only.

Even though Mack and Ryan wanted to go, my dad said no.

But Mack and Ryan were mad because they played Jr. Nuggets and they were good.

They were the "dynamic duo" in the sixth grade league and they said how I didn't even know how to play.

I didn't know how to play.

Not really.

But me and Zyler loved the Nuggets.

It was the only team I liked. The only one I even knew the players of and cared about.

Dad liked that I cared and he didn't let Mack and Ryan go.

Dad: You guys can watch it on TV.

Mack and Ryan: Logan can watch it on TV.

Dad: Stop pushing me or I won't pay for Elite.

So then they stopped pushing.

You can't push Dad too far and they wouldn't give up Elite summer basketball camp for anything. Not even upper-bowl playoff tickets with popcorn and Coke (because Mom wasn't there).

I went and it was okay.

But it was also weird.

Sort of like a charity case because I knew it was because of Zyler and me and everything and it didn't really help, and plus, I don't even know how to play.

Mom drives me home from Alta now.

The bus wasn't too bad.

In fact, at the beginning, it was almost all the way okay because most of the guys that were "The Ones" got rides with older brothers or sisters or neighborhood carpools.

My mom asked Patsy why hardly any of the boys rode the bus.

Patsy said the boys didn't like the bus or the old bus driver, who I heard was named Ben.

Patsy: We just don't trust the school bus system. You know, that old driver had it in for Brucey.

That's what she told Mom and that was it.

Except then Mom asked: What do you mean, out for him?

They were on the front porch.

Patsy: Well, that man kept harassing Brucey, so I called and complained and had Jack see what he could do. He has a lot of pull around here since he got that city chair.

That's all she said and Mom and Patsy were pretty good friends by then because of Dad and Jack playing NBA Live, but after awhile Mom said she wasn't sure what Patsy was up to.

Mom didn't know for sure if Patsy had "pure intentions."
Sometimes, she said, people will trick you. It takes a while to
get to know someone all the way.

A while like almost six months.

That's when Dad and Jack got in a fight and then Mom found
out for sure.

Now Mom drives me to school in the minivan on her way to
drop the others back at Mulholland because she thinks I can't
take care of myself.

She's [*whisper*] scared for me.

I don't care.

In the hall I see Laurel a lot.

And I won't look at her or anything because I don't want her to
think I am staring or anything like that.

But then one day I couldn't help it.

She came to school in a sequiny green dress thing and her brown
hair was all up or something.

Like she was in the movies.

She even had these clicky green sequiny heels that looked
really hard to walk in.

When she was walking down the hall with her backpack dragging
behind her on wheels, everyone sort of stepped back and stared.

A few people yelled stuff like: "Dork!" and "Yeah, right, Laurel. You wish." and "You're an idiot."

She kept walking and that was it.

I wrote this note to Laurel:

Wow
Gag
From Logan Paloney

But then I thought maybe she wouldn't know me or think it was dumb.

Plus, if you get caught in school with a note the teacher reads it out loud.

So I just ripped it up.

Once Bruce decided I was crapstock, for some reason everyone else thought I was crapstock too.

It was like a bomb.

It exploded, I mean, and everyone liked to say it.

"Crapstock."

Zyler and I weren't crapstock at Mulholland.

At least Zyler wasn't.

Maybe I was.

Maybe I was and I just didn't know it.

Here's how the crapstock bomb went off: I was outside because we had just moved in and I was sick of being inside and my mom and dad yelling for someone to bring something up and someone to bring something down.

I was also tired because my bike was at Mulholland still because I left it at me and Zyler's spot just in case.

So I hadn't really been riding around.

That meant I got tired very, very, very easily.

Our house on Judge was really big with a really big yard.

Much bigger than the Mulholland house with the strip of grass for Red light, Green light and hardly any front yard for Mom's tulips.

Judge was an upgrade.

So I was on the grass picking at it and resting when Bruce and

Luke and Toby came walking up. Except I didn't know they were Bruce and Luke and Toby yet.

Bruce: You just moved in.

Me: Uh-huh.

Luke: Why?

Me: What?

Luke: Why?

Me: Why what?

Bruce: Why did you move here, moron?

I was thinking and thinking and trying to think what to say.

Bruce: Hey, MOOORRRROOONNN, what's your problem?

Luke and Toby laughed and I didn't.

I just sat there.

Bruce: Well, that seals it, boys. We thought maybe someone cool was moving in but my hunch was right. You're crapstock. Once crapstock, always crapstock – can smell the moldy crap clear down the street.

And then I think they left.

I'm not sure because I don't remember all that well since I was crapstock.

At school I don't sit with anyone really.

I have friends:

Lael

Ricky

Shaun

Mark

Liza

Tallie

Those are the ones that are sort of my friends because of different reasons, like Lael and I have physics together and math club after school.

But that's it because he lives really far away and he only does school activities and he can't go to people's houses if it's not school- related.

At least that's what he told me when I invited him to sleep over once.

Ricky and Shaun are cool in my Life Skills class because we are the only boys and we sit together and laugh at Mrs. Shumway and her waddle.

But then I never see them again.

I think they have second lunch.

Mark is in my choir class and first lunch and he's okay, but I think he has mental problems because he doesn't really get what I say and he hates anything about aerodynamics or science or anything like that.

He mostly just likes to draw Manga.

Sometimes we talk about comic books but he really doesn't even know that much about them.

And Liza and Tallie are in my Sunday school class.

They're okay, but I don't really like to hang around with girls.

Except maybe Laurel.

She's pretty cool.

She's kind of like Cami in how I sort of like her.

Zyler and I both liked Cami, but in the way where you don't-really-talk-to-her like her.

And she knew because her friend Macy called us at Zyler's house when we were having a sleepover and asked which one of us it was.

No girls had ever called us and at first

Macy just said: Who likes Cami? You or Logan?

It was on speakerphone and we didn't even know who was talking.

Zyler: Well, who wants to know?

Macy: Just answer the question.

I shook my head at Zyler.

Zyler: I can't spill that kind of information unless I know who I'm dealing with.

Macy didn't say anything for a while because she was whispering or was muffled and then she said: It's Macy Clayton. Now answer the question.

Zyler looked at me and I shook my head again. There was no

right answer to the question and the whole thing was very shady.

Zyler: That information shall be forthcoming but not anytime soon. Please inquire at a later date.

Then he hung up.

Zyler: How did they know we were at my house?

And I didn't know how they knew.

We never went to Zyler's house for sleepovers because his dad was MEAN.

But this time we did because his dad had a job in Utah and wasn't going to be home for two days.

So it was just us and Zyler's twenty-year-old sister, Sharon-with-a-boyfriend, who was usually never there because she sort of lives with her boyfriend.

Me: I don't know how they knew.

Zyler: Maybe they were spying on us.

Me: Or maybe they were just calling you. Maybe they didn't know I was here.

Zyler: No. They knew. You could tell they knew. I bet they were spying on us – probably.

We ate some Cheetos that we'd got at the Minute Man down the street because Sharon gave us a ten and told us to shut up. She was cool sometimes but sometimes not.

So we ate the Cheetos and sort of talked about Cami and the phone call, but we didn't talk about it that much because we wanted to watch *Mystery Science Theater 3000*.

When Zyler fell asleep I started thinking about it again.

Who did Cami like? Maybe she liked me but more maybe she liked Zyler.

It probably wasn't me because I didn't really talk so much when girls or other people were around.

Mostly just when I was with Zyler.

But Zyler could talk when he wanted to. I mean if he felt like it, and he was pretty funny too.

And when you thought about it, Zyler had a sort of good-looking face.

It wasn't all the way good-looking but it was older-looking. And he had big green eyes that my mom called piercing – especially for his dark coloring, she would say.

And since I was regular with nothing really special on my face except freckles and usually sunburns.

Plus, I'd started to have a gut and that's why I hated going swimming because it would hang over sort of like Dad's, but not ten times as bad as Dad's.

So that's another reason I thought she probably liked Zyler.

But mostly Zyler didn't say that maybe she liked him or me more.

He just said it didn't matter.

And I thought he really meant it.

He said she was cute just like I did because of her red red ponytail and her different socks but he wasn't about to like like her.

Neither was I.

*

I wonder where Cami is now.

I wonder if she hates me as much as I think she does.

I heard her parents sent her to live with an aunt for a while in Detroit or Delaware or something.

If I were her I would move to Hong Kong.

Because sometimes you just want to be nowhere.

Or Hong Kong.

At the beginning of Christmas break Mom took me to the Reagan Towers downtown.

I thought we were going Christmas shopping for the others because they all had to stay home, but instead she took me to the Towers.

I'd never been there before and I had no idea what was going on.

But then we went in this office with *Dr. Jim Benson* on it and the Secretary said: Just one moment and he'll see you.

We sat down on a couch that was pretty nice but not really really nice.

It was a small office and there was a fish tank.

It seems like most doctors' offices have fish tanks and *Highlights* magazines.

Then a doctor came out of a door and said: Mrs. Paloney, why don't you step in first.

Mom got up and smoothed her round hair and walked into the office.

She said to me: I'll be right back.

Before, on the elevator, I had asked her: Where are we going?

She said: You'll see. It's no big deal but it's something we need.

Me: What do you mean?

She: Honey, just relax. This whole thing isn't just about you.

And then the bing of the elevator came and another guy got on and pushed eleven. We were going to ten and I couldn't talk to Mom while the guy was in there.

He had a big box of papers and he was wearing a suit even though he looked like a teenager.

At ten we got off and I didn't have time to say anything to Mom before the secretary and doctor, and then she was in the office.

I was almost going to ask the lady what kind of a doctor he was or where we were.

But I knew I wouldn't.

I just looked at the *Highlights*.

That was my first appointment with Dr. Jim Benson.

*

30

I just decided to write another note and I even gave it to Laurel.

To Laurel:
a few palindromes.
Pop
Level
From Logan (from your geography and pre-algebra classes)

Logan –
No duh about geog and algebra
Lion oil.
Laurel

I'm in a play at school.

It's pretty soon.

I tried out because they announced it in class and I thought maybe I would try out.

The play is *Peter Pan* and I got the part of a Lost Boy.

There are a lot of Lost Boys but I still got the part.

This is how I tried out: They said you had to go for three days after school and I wasn't going to do it because I didn't know how to act or even if I could sing.

You had to sing for this one.

Mom said I could sing.

In church I sang.

So I went to tryouts just to see what it was like.

And to see who was there.

No Bruce. No Luke. No Toby. No girls like Carmen or Vanessa or Mallory.

I didn't really know anyone except Laurel was there.

That's when I decided to just try it.

Just up and try it.

So I signed up and sat down in the auditorium seats with a whole bunch of other people I sort of knew but didn't and waited for my turn. When they got to the M's I was almost sick and throw-uppy. Lots of them knew how to sing really good and I did too, I said to myself.

And some weren't so good.

I was better than some for sure.

So then Michael Olsen went and he sang "Taps" – the song we sing in Scouts when we lower the flag. It was pretty good but he sang really shaky old-like. Like he was in an opera, and it sounded weird to me.

Then it was my turn.

Here's what happened when I tried out:

I got up there and there was a light on me.

Director People: What will you be singing?

Me: A hymn called "Where Can I Turn for Peace?"

Everyone watching: (whispering)

No one had sung a hymn or anything and I wasn't sure if you

were even allowed to – sing about God or anything. But I didn't know all the words to any other song.

Director People: Okay, go ahead.

And then I just sang it.

I was glad that there wasn't a piano or anything because then I could make it as high as I wanted and so I did.

And at first I sounded really bad.

I mean I thought I did, but no one was really laughing.

So I sang the whole thing.

I mean the whole first verse.

I didn't look up or anything.

I just sang.

I probably should have looked up because then they might have given me a part as a pirate or John or something.

But I didn't want to look up.

Director People after I sang:

Everyone watching:

Me:

I still was looking at the ground. Why wouldn't anyone say anything?

Director People: Okay, thank you.

And that was it.

After that day and another day of reading lines and another day of doing a dance I got a part.

I became a Lost Boy in the play *Peter Pan*.

*

When I found out I was in the play I wanted to maybe get in shape.

That's why I drank a weight-loss shake, and it wasn't too bad.

I was down in my room so no one would see.

Especially not Mack or Ryan.

The play was in two months, at the end of May, and maybe I could lose some weight by then.

I wonder if Zyler would've thought a play was dumb.

He probably would've liked it. Especially since he would have been a lead part like Captain Hook, I bet.

Because of the play and because of Scouts, I think Mom and Dad thought I was okay.

I never told them about Bruce or Toby or Luke.

They thought we were friends maybe.

They thought things were better.

After the thing with Zyler, I was alone and I wouldn't leave my room.

And.

I.

Was.

Sad.

So they thought I had friends at Judge.

At first.

But then they figured it out.

They were already worried about me enough and Mom had the pregnancy and Dad had the new mortgage and there were so many things.

I was always the one they were worried worried worried about and I was always the one I heard them talking talking talking about.

They thought Judge was the answer to everything and Zyler.

I sort of wanted them to think that, too, so I tried not to stay in my room so long and I talked more and I did Scouts and I told Mom I was fine.

I didn't want them to know about Bruce or Toby or Luke.

Mom says I should hang out with Mack and Ryan.

She sometimes comes in my room and says things like: They love you and they want to hang out with you.

Me:

Mom: You guys used to go play basketball and run around.

Me: Not really.

Mom: Yes.

Me:

Mom: And Ryan was just saying the other day how much he wished you would do stuff with the two of them more.

I knew she was making that up. Ryan and Mack didn't need me. They did everything together and they were always doing sports or talking to Dad about the NBA or NFL or NHL. Or about how they got in trouble at school. Dad would act mad but then I knew he thought they were maybe cool like him.

So I said to Mom: I'm fine.

But I know she didn't leave it alone because a couple hours later Ryan comes walking in my room without even knocking.

Ryan: What's up, dork?

Me: Nothing.

Ryan: Why do you sit down here all the time?

Me: Where's Mack?

Ryan: Helping Dad with something.

Me:

Ryan:

Me:

Ryan: Okay. I think I'm going to go back upstairs.

And then he left.

*

When we were younger Ryan fell out of a tree and broke his arm. It was only the three of us at home and I was in charge and we didn't know what to do.

Ryan was bawling and bawling: It hurts so bad. I can't move it. It hurts so bad.

Mack was just sitting next to him in the grass staring at the bone.

At first I didn't know what to do.

I was scared.

But then I did this:

I told Ryan it was going to be okay.

I told Mack to talk to Ryan rather than just sit and stare.

I called Mom on her cell but she didn't answer.

I called Dad at work but he didn't answer.

And then I called 911 and said: My brother has fallen out of a tree and I think he broke his arm.

I was outside on the cordless phone and the lady told me what to do:

To see if he was in shock.

To see if he was bleeding.

To see if he was cold.

To see if it hurt anywhere else.

I said: Ryan, you have to stop crying, okay?

And he did.

And then I checked for everything.

Mom came home right then and we all went to the hospital and it was going to be okay.

While we were in the waiting room Mack said: It's a good thing Logan was there.

Mom looked at me and smiled.

That's how I used to be.

Now I don't do anythin

To Laurel:
Rat star
From: Logan

Logan –
Oh, cameras are macho
Laurel.

Here's how I met Zyler: At school in Mrs. Frazier's fourth grade class.

Here's why: We were made partners for a diorama project where you have to re-create an old village or civilization in a big cardboard box with sticks and action figures and stuff and then write a report on the people.

Here's what I was when I found out my assignment: Sort of scared.

Here's why: Zyler moved in in the middle of the year and he was so tough because you could just tell.

I mean, he wore T-shirts that had all these bands on them and I don't know any bands or anything, and he also had some really funny T-shirts that said things like "Get out of my face, bucket of nerd pus." And on it was this huge bucket with green and yellow stuff coming out of it, plus stuff like broken eyeglasses and bow ties.

And at recess he didn't play kickball or anything.

He just drew stuff.

Or he'd run really fast around the playground over and over.

He was the fastest in our grade for sure.

And pretty strong – forty-seven pull-ups in the presidential PE challenge.

I could do four.

So at first none of us guys ever talked to him really.

But the girls did.

Girls always liked Zyler.

So anyway, Mrs. Frazier assigned us together for the diorama and I was going to ask her to switch me but then Zyler came up to me and said: So what should we do it on?

Me:

Zyler:

Me:

Zyler:

Me:

Zyler:

Me: I don't know.

Zyler: What about on the Japanese samurai?

We were best friends ever since.

Until now.

*

Dad keeps talking about Scouts.

And even Mack and Ryan talk about it.

I don't.

Yesterday I drank another one of my mom's weight-loss shakes.

Actually, they're not really hers.

She doesn't need weight-loss shakes because she's about to have the baby, but my dad does so she buys them and then she never says she got them for him because Dad gets mad or "self-conscious."

Mom told me that awhile ago when we were at Costco and she was buying them.

Me: Why are you getting those?

Mom: They're delicious.

Me: Are you trying to lose weight?

Mom: Maybe.

And I was suspicious because even though we could never get Coke or Twinkies or good stuff like that, she usually lets us have raisin oatmeal cookies or the chicken wings with ranch or some normal stuff.

This time she said no.

No junk whatsoever.

Just the usual no-sugar cereals, soy milk, spinach, apples, and fish.

But then weight-loss shakes?

41

Me: Are these for me?

She stopped the cart and looked all serious at me.

Mom: Logan, no. Are you kidding? You're a growing boy.

Me: Mmmph?.?.?.

Mom: Do you think you need to lose weight? Do you feel fat?

Me: No, Mom. Sheesh.

Two girls walked by looking at us. Crapstock.

Mom: Well, you're not. You're not fat. You are a growing boy.

Me: Hmmph.

Mom: These are for your dad. He's eating way too much these days and it's not good for him.

Me: Okay.

I didn't want to talk about the stupid drinks anymore.

Mom: Haven't you noticed?

I didn't say anything.

Mom: Your father is very self-conscious these days. He's even getting private around me and that's really big for your father.

Gross. Gross and I wanted her to just stop talking.

But she wouldn't.

Mom: We can't tell him these are for him. He really is acting strange. The other night he couldn't stop talking about his weight and his?.?.?.

I cut her off.

Me: Mom – I have to go use the bathroom.

And I was gone.

*

I thought I maybe saw Cami's dad in the parking lot of Costco
so I tried to hide.
I know he hates me like he hates Zyler.
He probably thinks we're the same.

After Costco, my mom and I saw Bruce and Toby and Luke and
girls like Carmen and Vanessa and Mallory at the mall.
She saw them first and then I saw them.
We walked faster and they didn't even know we were there.
Mom is pretty cool sometimes.

Laurel is a pirate in *Peter Pan*.
She looked up when she sang.
And she has a really pretty voice.
She has to wear a lot of dark makeup around her eyes for the part.
She does it even though we aren't close to dress rehearsal or
anything like that.
It helps her get into character.
I heard her tell Ms. March that.
Some people think it's kind of dumb – "overboard like always,"
they say.

43

But

Ms. March said to Laurel: Good for you, Laurel.

I don't know what a Lost Boy wears yet.

Zyler's dad has tattoos on his arms.

But I know that tattoos don't mean you're bad.

My uncle Phil has tattoos all over the place and he's the best uncle. He isn't married and he always goes all over on trips to take pictures for different magazines. Whenever he visits he has the coolest stories and stuff to give us.

His tattoos are cool.

Zyler's dad's aren't.

He's an electrician and if he wants he can make a lot of money.

He has a big big big truck.

He's mad all the time but Zyler says not all all the time.

He swears a lot.

He hates it when you talk when he's watching TV or when you leave the light on anywhere.

He really hates lights on.

He lives with Zyler and sometimes Sharon and he always brought different girls home and Zyler always wanted to sleep over at our house because he hated it there – mostly.

Sometimes he could sleep over and sometimes he couldn't.

Sometimes his dad wanted him to stay and get drinks and food for all his friends and to be there in case they needed more.

Or sometimes he just wanted him to stay because?.?.?.

Zyler's dad: You're my freaking son and you'll do what the freak I say.

Only he doesn't go soft and say "freak."

Here's when I met Zyler's dad: Not for a long time until like the summer after fourth.

Here's why: When we had to do the diorama thing, we always did it at my house. Zyler said we couldn't go over to his or anything.

Zyler even lived really close to me and we'd ride bikes to school or walk home, but I still never went inside his house.

But then one day in the summer Zyler said: We can hang out at my house if you want.

Me: Okay.

The reason we could I found out was because Zyler's dad was gone on a contract for three days and Sharon-with-a-boyfriend was going to the lake with her friends.

Zyler: My family is sort of weird.

Me: Oh.

Zyler: That's why it's better to come here only if no one is home.

Me: Okay.

The house was sort of really messy with stuff all over.

Not like our house and the chores and can't leave for school until your bed is made.

But there was also all this expensive stuff like sound equipment and a motor from a car his dad was working on and then all these trophies.

There was one really big trophy.

Me: Whoa, what is that for?

Zyler: That's Dad's motocross trophy.

So Zyler's house was pretty cool.

And Zyler really wanted me to come over so I could see his new flying squirrel.

Zyler: My dad got it from this breeder guy for, like, three hundred bucks.

Me: Three hundred bucks? Are you serious?

Zyler: Yeah, and he said he'll buy a girl for it and we can sell the babies if I want.

Me: That's sick.

Zyler: What is?

Me: Making the squirrels do it and everything.

Zyler: It's not sick – it's money, man.

And I guess yeah. But I still thought it was sick.

Zyler had the squirrel, an iguana, a boa constrictor, and a cat that we both hated because it was so stupid, but it was Sharon's cat.

I couldn't believe how much stuff Zyler had and the pets and

the posters and the CDs and the video games with his own TV
in his room and everything.

Me: Your room is so awesome. I can't believe your dad lets you
have all this stuff and pets and everything.

Zyler: Yeah. It's pretty cool.

But just then we heard a loud something pull up. And it was
Zyler's dad in his big big big truck.

Zyler looked out the window and then said: Crap, you gotta go.
He's home early and he doesn't look good.

Me: What?

Zyler: You gotta get out of here.

But I didn't get it and I had the iguana on my neck and so I tried
to hurry but then that's when I met Zyler's dad.

And he was yellow eyeballs and hitting the wall.

He was mad at Zyler for some reason I didn't understand.

And he told me to get the hell out of their house.

I found out later that sometimes Zyler's dad was okay.

But most of the time not okay.

Almost never okay.

Practically never okay.

But there was one other time, and this really is true, when Zyler
called me and this?—

Zyler: Hey, what are you doing?

Me: Nothing.

Zyler: Well, my dad wants to take us to the Nickelcade. Can you go?

Me: Really?

Zyler: Yeah, and I bet he'll take us to eat after. He's in a really good mood and he said we can stay as long as we want.

Me: I don't know.

Zyler: Please, Logan. He said you could come. He even said to invite you and he's really good at pinball. You should see him.

Me: Okay. I'll see if I can and then come over.

But then I went upstairs with my coat on and Mom saw me and: Where are you going?

I thought about lying but I didn't and then Mom said: No way. I'm not letting you go anywhere alone with that man.

Me: Come on, Mom. Just this once.

Mom: No way.

So I didn't get to go.

Zyler said his dad got the high score on all the pinball machines plus Mortal Kombat, Rad Racer, and Metroid. The highest score of all at the Nickelcade.

*

Not everything in Scouts was bad.

We did a lot of different things and some of them I really liked.
Like KNOTS.

I can do a water knot, a munter hitch, a square knot, and a
bowline knot.

I can do all of these faster and better than anyone else.

Jack was impressed.

Jack: Wow, Logan. You are our knot expert. Look at this, guys.

The six other guys, including you-know-whos, looked at me and
at my rope.

Bruce: So what?

Jack: Bruce, look at your rope and then look at Logan's. Keep
your mouth shut if you can't back it up.

Bruce shrugged. He didn't even get the clove hitch, let alone
the prussic.

That day was probably the best in Scouts.

And it was in the beginning.

Like our second pack meeting, so Jack thought I was pretty
smart and maybe a good Scout. I was glad because I thought that
might keep Bruce and them away from me.

But Jack liking me didn't really last.

Bruce is too smart for that.

*

I couldn't believe it.

Dr. Benson in the Towers was a trap.

After Mom went in there for a while and I had been sitting there staring at fish because *Highlights* sucked, Dr. Jim Benson came out and said: Logan, why don't you come join us.

The room was like this:

A big window with a view of the mountains.

A big desk with everything set out on it very even.

A chair for the doctor that was like what you'd think.

Two leather chairs and one my mom was in.

A couch over by another door that was maybe for a bathroom.

Pictures of smiling dogs and kids and Ansel Adams photos all over.

Books.

I sat down.

Dr. Benson: Logan, do you know why you are here?

Me: No.

Dr. Benson: Okay. That's what your mother told me.

Me:

Dr. Benson: I'm a counselor.

Me:

Dr. Benson: Your parents thought it'd be a good idea if you and I talked now and then.

Me:

No way no way no way no way no way no way no way no way no way no way

Dr. Benson: Would that be okay with you?

I looked at my mom. She nodded and smiled.

Unbelievable.

Dr. Benson: It's your turn to talk now, Logan.

Me:

Mom: Honey, it's okay.

Me:

I had to get out of there.

Mom: Honey?

She was staring at me and tried to take my hand. I moved away.

Me:

Dr. Benson: You know what? It's okay. You don't have to talk this first time.

Me:

Dr. Benson: How about I'll just talk.

And then he stared at me and stared at me and then finally

Dr. Benson: My name is Dr. Jim Benson and I am forty-eight years old. I have three children and I love baseball and eating. I also like to go boating. Have you ever been boating before, Logan?

Unbelievable.

Mom: Umm, no. We don't have a boat or anything. But he has been down a river before, haven't you, Logan?

*

That's when I got up and walked out. I just walked out.

I didn't stop in the waiting room either. I didn't stop in the hall. I didn't stop down in the lobby. I didn't even stop at the car. I just kept going. But soon I was running. I sort of ran up the hill.

A hill.

I didn't know where I was exactly except that we were by the university, but it didn't matter. I ran up a hill and there was a construction site there and a bunch of guys jackhammering.

I ran past them.

I felt stupid for all of them to see me running but I didn't stop.

I kept running and panting and almost dying until I passed them and got to the base of the mountain. I can't really describe where I was or what it was like because I didn't know and I was about to pass out.

All I know was that all of a sudden I was at the base of the mountains where the trails start and I sat down by a tree where no one was around and no one could see me from the road.

I sat down and then

I yelled.

*

Laurel is pretty funny in class.

She doesn't really say things but she laughs at weird times and sometimes she hums.

Everyone will look at her but she just keeps humming.

Girls like Carmen and Vanessa and Mallory think she's "super dorky."

I know because I heard them say that – "super dorky."

I don't know why she does all that weird stuff, but I think she's funny.

To Laurel:
U.F.O. tofu
From Logan

Logan –
I am A. I.
Tel Aviv erases a revival. E. T.
Laurel

Here's how Zyler was: Brave.

Brave like once, when we didn't even know where his dad was, Zyler started the dirt bike his dad had in the garage. We'd always wanted to ride it, but we knew we couldn't even ask.

But one day we were eating Froot Loops on my front porch and it was hot and boring and there was nothing to do.

So Zyler said: I don't even care.

Before I could think what he'd said, he was already on his bike.

I ran to catch up and soon we were at his dirt-yard house.

Me: What are we doing?

Zyler: I'm bored and he never even rides it.

Me: You're not saying what I think you're saying.

He smiled at me and said: Are you scared?

And yes, yes I was sort of scared.

Me: I don't know.

Zyler: I knew it. You got to get over it, Paloney. You got to live.

He laughed and so did I. It was a line from our favorite movie, *Destinos*, and it was supposed to be our motto – sort of. If we had one.

54

So we went in the garage.

Me: Are you going to take it out on the street?

Zyler: I don't know yet. I'm not sure if it has gas.

Me: I don't think we should take it out there. What if your dad comes home?

Zyler: I'm sick of my dad.

I looked at him and he seemed serious. He usually wasn't serious.

Me: Yeah, but what if he found out?

Zyler: He'd kick the crap out of me.

And he really, really would.

Me: Then why are we doing this?

Zyler: Then why wouldn't we do this? What are we supposed to do? Sit on the front porch eating soggy cereal all day?

Me: Yeah, yeah we could do that all day. It's better than getting the crap kicked out of us.

Zyler: Logan, you don't need to worry. He won't touch you.

It was true. Zyler's dad had yelled yelled yelled at me but he had never hit me or anything.

Zyler, however, was a different story. A very different story.

He had a lot of "household accidents":

a broken arm.

a broken collarbone.

stitches eight times.

a couple of black eyes.

and bruises.

So we went in the garage and there it was: his dad's dirt bike. And it wasn't the biggest bike or anything but it was really cool. Like fast and loud cool and we'd looked at it a ton of times.

Zyler opened the door to the backyard.

Zyler: I'm just going to ride it out back and then back in. Then you can if you want.

I didn't want.

He went to the side of the bike where it leans on the kickstand and threw his leg over the lowest part of the seat.

I couldn't believe he was doing this.

I tried to hear if anything was coming down the street.

Anything.

Zyler was having a hard time getting it started or something. But when he finally kicked the kickstand back up, a black cloud belched out the exhaust pipe.

He pulled a lever by his left hand and tapped down with his left foot.

Dirt bike: Vroom put put Vroom (or something like that)

The garage funneled the sound of the motor. Then the bike jumped and sputtered out.

Zyler: I can't get the clutch to work.

Me: I have no idea how to work that thing.

Zyler: It's not that hard – see, you just pull the choke, pull back on the throttle once, and kick down on the starter.

Me:

So then he did it again.

This time the motor revved and revved and didn't sputter out.

Zyler yelling: Oh my crap, this is so awesome!

Me yelling back: Yeah!

Zyler still yelling – the motor was really loud: I'm going to take it in the backyard!

Me: Okay!

And then I watched him go out the back door of the garage. He sort of jumped at first, but then he was really riding it. He was really riding it, and it was really loud.

I followed him out there and watched him ride around and around their weedy, trashy dump-yard lot.

He was screaming and laughing and I had a stomachache worrying his dad would get home, but then I watched him almost pop a wheelie and then I was screaming and laughing.

We were out there for almost an hour or so: It was so long.

But it was fun and awful and better than I thought.

I mean, I didn't drive the bike but I did sit on back a couple times and we fell over and everything.

It was so cool.

His dad never found out. At least not really that I knew.

Sometimes Zyler didn't tell me everything with his dad, but when I asked he said his dad never knew.

I'd never do stuff like that if my dad was like that, but I guess you got to live.

*

Another time Zyler said this: My dad isn't what you think.

Me:

Zyler: He bought me this.

And he showed me his Casio G-Shock watch and said how they'd gone for pizza and drinks and he could order whatever he wanted but he just got a strawberry lemonade and he even got dessert.

Me:

Zyler: He's my dad, Log.

Me: Okay.

Zyler: You still don't get it.

Me:

Zyler: He's all I got.

Me: Okay.

Sometimes, before it happened and everything, I'd ride by Cami's house all by myself.

I'd do it early with my paper route.

Those times I didn't tell Zyler about.

I didn't think he'd care anyway, probably.

But then again, maybe he would.

I didn't really know anything.

*

After I ran away from Dr. Benson's office and I yelled and just sat there, I knew I was going to be in trouble.

I knew Mom and Dad were going to be mad.

I just hoped they wouldn't call the police.

They called the police the one time I ran away at Mulholland.

But that was clear back when I was eleven and I was mad because Mom had read my journal.

And she'd found out about how Zyler and I had stolen a couple candy bars from Beeman's and she was so MAD.

I remember coming home from school the day she found out and she

Yelled this: Logan Freeman Paloney, you get in here right now!

She was in the kitchen and I had no idea what this was going to be about.

With Mom you never knew.

Mom: Mr. Beeman called.

Me: Okay.

Mom: Don't you get sarcastic with me, young man.

Me:

Mom: He told me that you and Zyler have taken some things from his store.

At this point I was confused.

There was no way Mr. Beeman had really called because Zyler had taken the bars back because we felt so bad and he apologized and said sorry for me too.

I couldn't go because it was dinnertime and so I had to be home.

Zyler doesn't really have a curfew.

Mr. Beeman was pretty nice about it and actually gave them back to Zy for his honesty. This had all happened like a few months before this encounter with Mom.

Me: What are you talking about, Mom?

Mom: Logan. Stop lying. I know the truth.

Me: No you don't, and you're lying.

Mom: You're grounded.

Me: That's not fair.

Mom: You are grounded, young man, and that's it.

And then she started talking about the neighbors finding out and what about Mr. Beeman and on and on.

Later that night when I was sitting pissed on my bed I saw that my journal was the wrong side in on my shelf. I pulled it out and read my last entry.

March 18

Zyler and I took candy bars from Beeman's. We both feel bad. Zyler will fix it.

That's all I had written and I hadn't opened the book since.

Mom had read my journal.

I was so mad and mad and mad that I decided I didn't want a liar for a mom.

So I packed my pillowcase and snuck out the back door.

That was the worst runaway I've ever done so far.

And that's when I found out for real about Zyler's dad.

*

I ran away because my mom lied and read my journal.

I went to Zyler's.

Here's what I saw when I climbed into his window: Nothing.

Zyler wasn't in there, but his light was on and his music was on and his clothes were all over just like always.

Here's what I did: Listen to see if I could hear him in the hall or bathroom.

Here's what I heard: _____ except the TV sort of.

Here's what I did next: Started to climb back out the window because I didn't want to be there if only Zyler's dad was there because maybe Zyler had to go get him something. Right when I touched the ground is when it happened.

Here's what I heard: A scream. A "No, Dad! Please, no!!" And it was Zyler and it was so loud and shaking and backed into a corner. "NO NO NO!!! PLEASE!!!"

Here's what I heard next: Shut up! Shut up you (&*%^% (&*)!!! And his voice was deep and down deep and I could almost feel it deep.

Here's next: Please?! Please?.?.?.

And it was almost a whimper and I wanted him to stop but I couldn't do anything.

I just stood outside the window and heard it. I mean I couldn't do anything because I wasn't even in the house and I didn't know where they were and I had to go.

Then: Scream scream scream. Pound pound pound.

That's when I didn't know what to do so I left and I forgot my pillowcase because I left so fast.

I'm sorry, Zyler.

I'm so sorry. For everything.

I didn't go all the way home after that.

I just went to this secret spot me and Zyler have that's under our huge pine tree by the chain-link fence. You can't see in from the outside, but if you go under the branches there's a cave sort of before the branches get thick.

I went to our spot and tried to breathe.

I couldn't.

And I thought maybe I should go back to Zyler's, but I knew I -couldn't go back but I should go back, but then Zyler would be mad but then I left my pillowcase and he'd know I was there and he'd want to know why I was there and what I saw and I didn't want him to know.

I didn't see anything.

I wasn't really there.

And so then I heard the sirens because Mom and Dad were looking for me and they couldn't find me.

I came out when the cops came and Mom grabbed me and was crying: Don't ever do that again. Don't ever do that again.

Mom and Dad were both hugging me and hugging me.

But then Mom grounded me again even though she already had and I felt so dumb that the cops were there.

Them: We are so sorry, Officer.

Me:

Officer: It's all right. Slow night anyway. You keep out of trouble, young man. Quit making your parents worry.

Me:

Mom: Say thank you to the officers, Logan.

Me: Thank you.

And that was it.

They both wanted to know everything. Where had I been. What was going on.

I told them I was in the back the whole time.

Dad: Didn't you hear us yelling?

Me: No.

Mom: Are you sure?

Me: NO.

They looked at each other and then told me to go to bed.

I didn't say anything to Zyler either.

And he didn't ask, which I was glad about.

Except he said: You left your pillowcase in my room.

Me: Yeah.

Zyler: Stuff fell out and I'm borrowing your Trekkie T-shirt.

Me: Okay.

Us:

And that was it.

*

I liked Cami before Zyler did.

I know that because the day Zyler first saw her, he said: Wow, who is that?

And I said: Cami Wakefield.

I knew Cami because her mom and my mom used to do yoga with DVDs together.

Always at our house because at Cami's house there was no TV, and she didn't even care, she said.

It was when I was a kid and it wasn't for so long because then Mom decided yoga was bad for her back and so she started doing Tai Chi, but I guess Cami's mom didn't want to do Tai Chi.

So whenever Cami's mom came over so did Cami.

She was an only child and that made it so she never had to be in charge of anyone.

I didn't play with girls or anything but I had to with Cami, Mom said.

But it was okay because Cami wasn't like other girls.

She was different.

Like she hated flies so bad she would make big huge plans on how to kill them complete with attack positions and everything.

And she had this fire red hair that was never just right but always sticking out around and around. Sometimes she'd make me do beauty parlor when she came over, and I felt so dumb but it was funny with the hair spray and all over and then she did mine with food coloring once to see if it would dye and I got in big trouble.

She wore different color kinds of socks every day and the main thing was her eyes: Sort of too far apart but bright blue.

I'd never seen eyes so blue before.

And then Zyler said: Wow, who is that?

And I said: Cami Wakefield.

And then, instead of just not doing anything like me (I hadn't talked to Cami since the yoga stopped), Zyler yelled: Hey, redhead, what's your name?

That was near the end of sixth grade when we were hanging around the playground and Cami and her friend Macy were swinging or something.

Cami: What?

Zyler: What's your name?

Cami: Ask your friend.

They started laughing and then rode away on their bikes.

Zyler: How come I've never seen her before?

Me: Because she goes to the Waterford – the private school.

Zyler: But she lives by us?

Me: They have the biggest house in the neighborhood – on Oak.

After that was when we started riding past Cami Wakefield's house.

Cami started going to our junior high last year in seventh.

We saw her more then.

A lot more than now.

*

So the next time at Scouts was okay. I mean the time after knots. I can barely remember what we did really. I just remember being relieved because no one talked to me: not Bruce, not Luke, and not Toby.

Not even Jack.

Good.

But then the time after that is when Jack started to hate me.

We were in Bruce and Jack's backyard and we were supposed to be learning how to make a fire without matches or lighters.

Since they have this huge backyard plus a sort of dirt field, Jack had us all build our own pits.

It was hard work because Jack didn't want anything to get started on fire or ruin his delphiniums or new deck and the Jacuzzi or anything. So we had to dig big holes for our fire.

Bruce was mad: Dad, when are we going to have steel wool and batteries in the wilderness?

Jack: That's why you pack them with you, Bruce.

Bruce: Why don't I just pack a lighter or matches or something?

Jack: They could get wet; now shut up and get going on your fire.

Bruce: You shut up.

And then Jack got pissed at Bruce.

Really pissed and said: Hey, smart-ass, one more word out of you?.?.?.

Bruce sort of made a face but Jack saw so he threw his Scout manual at Bruce.

Jack:

Bruce:

Jack went inside to cool down and everyone else was quiet.

Bruce acted like he didn't care. That the book didn't hurt him even if he had a big red mark on his face.

That's when he came over to me.

Bruce: How's the pit going?

Me:

Bruce: Hey, crapstock, are you deaf?

Me:

I just kept digging and making my pit.

Bruce: I know about you.

Me:

My heart started going fast and sweating.

Bruce: I know what happened at your last school.

By now the others had stopped digging. I didn't look up. Please, no. Please.

Bruce: You're dirty. You're dirty dirty dirty crapstock.

Me:

Bruce: Yeah, my mom told me all about it after your mom called before you guys even moved here.

Dig dig dig dig dig dig dig dig dig dig dig dig dig dig dig dig dig dig

Bruce: Mom said to be nice but not too nice. Don't get too close to boys like you. She said not to tell anyone either, but I think it's time to tell. Don't you, crapstock?

Toby and Luke were standing behind him.

Bruce: You never know what you might do – you MOLESTER.

Me:

I couldn't breathe I couldn't move I couldn't think I couldn't do anything anything anything anything anything anything anything anything anything anything anything.

So then he was right there in my face.

Bruce: Did you hear me? You M-O-L-E-S-T-E-R.

And that's when I snapped.

I hit him as hard as I could with the shovel. But it wasn't so hard because I sort of missed because he was too close or something. But everyone screamed and Bruce fell.

And I jumped on him and he was pushing me off or trying to.

And there was Luke and Toby but I don't know what else and dirt in my mouth and I was bigger and I was shoving his face into the ground and they were screaming fightfightfightfight fightfight fightfightfightfightfightfightfightfightfightfightfight fight!

That's when Jack came out and that's when I balled up and Bruce was yelling and everyone was yelling and I was crying and crying and that wasn't the first time or the last time.

Jack hated me after that and so did everyone else who didn't already.

*

That night I slept almost twenty-four hours.

Almost all Saturday.

I've done that before and I could sleep longer if Mom would let me.

To Laurel:
Go do dog
From Logan

Logan—
Go deliver a dare, vile dog.
Laurel.

To Laurel:
Straw warts
From Logan

*

Back in seventh grade I called Cami once.

Actually twice.

Three times.

But I usually hung up.

But she had caller ID and once she called back.

I said I wanted to know about an assignment in math because we had that together.

Cami: What did you want to know?

Me: It's about exponents.

Cami: I don't know so much about them.

Me: Oh.

Cami: Is that it?

Me: I don't know.

Cami: Well, I better go.

Me: Yeah. I have to too.

Sometimes I think about everything and

I

Am

So

Sorry.

*

At play practice I usually just stand on the sides.

I don't have any lines or anything but I still have to go because everyone has to go to the big rehearsals.

The private ones for Wendy and Peter Pan and John and Captain Hook happen after the big ones or during lunch.

When it's my turn to come on, a bunch of us come out of a tree – it's not there yet – and we run around Peter and sing with him.

It's sort of dumb, but then I sort of like it too.

One rehearsal Ms. March said: Okay, okay, everyone. We need some volunteers to work on the set. The crew is behind and the tree house is a disaster – no offense, Sam [Sam's in charge of the set].

Sam: It's okay.

Ms. March: Mr. Jeffries volunteered to start over on a tree house if we can finagle a special team. Are there any volunteers?

The cast:

Ms. March: Anyone?

The cast:

Then Laurel raised her hand.

Ms. March: Thank you, Laurel. Now who else?

I didn't really want to volunteer. I mean, the rehearsals alone were taking way too much time and everything.

But I raised my hand.

Ms. March: Okay, and Logan. Good. We need about two more.

Three more guys and one girl volunteered. Ms. March was very happy.

I tried to look at Laurel but she wasn't looking at me so I didn't look at her.

I like her nose, her pirate makeup, and the way she stuffs her hair on the back of her head?.?.?.?and the palindromes.

But she didn't have a swayey walk or anything.

Logan:
Doc, note, I dissent. A fast never prevents a fatness.
I diet on cod.
Laurel

To Laurel:
DNA land
From Logan

Dad got a raise.
He's happy.
Mom's happy.
Mack and Ryan are happy.

72

Mom says the baby in her stomach is happy.

And I don't care really.

No one came to find me after Dr. Benson's appointment.

I just sat there.

I sat and sat and sat there.

There wasn't anything I could think of to do or to think or to say.

I just sat and tried to be totally blank.

No nothing.

No Bruce, No Luke, No Toby, No Judge, No Alta, No NBA Live, No Cami Wakefield, No Dr. Benson, and especially No Zyler.

It was hard.

But this is how I did it.

I thought about if I ever got in an accident it would be okay.

I wouldn't want to die, I didn't think.

It would be better if I was in a coma.

A coma for a few months.

At least until after school got out.

Or it might be better if I was in a coma for three years.

I wonder if your brain keeps developing while you're in a coma because I'd want to be ready to graduate from high school when I got out of it.

So I'd have to have been still thinking or else I wouldn't be able to pass.

I bet Mom would read to me.

If she had time without the kids and her friends and her cramps from her pregnancy and Dad and their dates and sick stuff and everything.

She could also get those CDs that teach you Spanish and Japanese and Russian. Those would be the three I would like to learn while I was in a coma.

I'd just lie there and listen.

She could also get some astronomy books, and I wonder if they do physics books on CD.

It would be hard to explain the equations.

And I could have a physical therapist that would work me out every day. They would help me lift weights and do cardio in the pool even though I was in a coma. I think they do that.

And people would feel so bad and would stop stop stop.

And I think Laurel would visit me and bring my homework and tell me about how the play is going and say some palindromes and maybe we would watch videos together and she could hold my hand.

No, that was weird.

Because I'd be unconscious.

But she could come and visit.

*

I was still thinking about the coma when I heard people shouting my name.

People like my mom and dad and Mack and Ryan.

I didn't get how they found out where I was.

I had run and run and run.

And why were they all there?

I stayed quiet for a while and listened to them wanting to find me. I wanted them to find me.

I wanted to find me.

And then I gave up.

I mean, and then I gave myself up.

When I finally let everyone find me, Mom was crying.

Dad just hugged me and so did the twins.

That night we had pizza and Coke and Twinkies.

Mom bought it and we all looked at her to see if she was going crazy, but she just smiled and said it was a special occasion.

A Zyler occasion.

I couldn't believe she said that.

I don't think anyone could believe it.

But then Mack said: Mom, what do you mean by that?

Mom: Zyler loved Twinkies and Coke and I know I never let you guys have it. But today is a special Zyler occasion.

Me: Why?

Mom: Because I think it's time that we started talking about him and remembering.

Everyone:

Mom: Who wants pepperoni?

Everyone:

Dad: I'll have one.

Mom: I'll have one too.

Mack: Me too.

Soon everyone was eating except me. This was too weird for me. Too weird. Too weird. It wasn't like Zyler was dead or something.

Zyler was pretty strong, like in everything. Like how he never ever cried.

Well, almost never.

Mom and Dad keep asking if I want them to find out – if I want to call him or talk to him.

He e-mailed once and then never again.

I think maybe he doesn't feel like talking to me.

*

The first day I went to the *Peter Pan* set-making thing, I realized I was in the wrong place.

I thought it was going to be backstage but I guess it was in the drama room.

So I was going to leave.

But then, right when I really was going to leave, I heard some people talking. But it wasn't just anybody talking. It was Toby and Laurel.

I think.

Toby: What does this note mean?

Laurel: Give it back – it's none of your business.

Toby: DNA land? Is this some kind of code?

Laurel: It's nothing. Give it back.

Toby: Are you swapping DNA with him?

Laurel: Shut up, Toby. You are so disgusting. Give it back.

Toby: He's not what he seems. He's not some quiet nerd. He's sick.

Laurel: Why are you talking to me, anyway? You haven't talked to me since fifth grade.

Toby: Because this is important. You don't know about him and we're trying to make sure we protect EVERYONE.

Laurel: Who's we?

Toby: Us, the guys.

Laurel: Who? You and Luke and your master, Bruce? You guys are so stupid.

I was holding my breath. Holding. Holding and standing back

behind a big black block they use for walls sometimes.

Toby: Look, I'm just warning you. Believe me, you need to be warned. Everyone does. Especially girls. You don't know what he did to a girl at his last school.

no no no no no no no no no no no no no no no no no

Laurel: I'm sure it was totally awful.

Me:

Toby: Fine, at least I warned you. But when you want to know more, come find me. Here's your stupid note. If I were you, I'd stay away from him – I mean it.

And then he left. Laurel took a deep breath and then she left too.

I didn't leave.

After I heard Laurel and Toby leave the stage, I just stood there behind the side curtain for a really long time.

How did he see the note?

What should I do?

Should I do something?

Maybe they thought it was from someone else.

Or maybe I heard them wrong.

Or maybe nothing.

I knew they were talking about me. I knew it because I'd been hearing it for weeks.

I'd been hearing Bruce and Luke and Toby whispering and pointing and laughing and spitting at me.

And I didn't know exactly what they were saying, but then I knew exactly what they were saying.

I couldn't run away from it even though I wanted to and my parents wanted me to and I wanted me to and everyone wanted me to.

It was here.

I sat down on the floor.

On the black floor of the stage, and I didn't cry.

Because I just sat there and thought about being nowhere and no one.

Or in a coma.

But then this:

Logan—
Dr. Awkward.
NO TRACE, NOT ONE CARTON
Laurel.

Why did she put it in caps?

Dr. Awkward? No trace?

What was she trying to say?

I didn't write back.

I decided I wasn't going to make sets.

I wasn't going to be in the play.

Maybe I wasn't even going to go to school.

But then the next day I still went to school and I still went to the rehearsal.

Even though I don't know why.

But I wasn't going to go to the set thing and Laurel could throw up and die if she wanted and I wouldn't care and I hated everyone and I would not show my face at set making and I didn't know why she wrote Dr. Awkward and then NO TRACE, NOT ONE CARTON. If she was trying to say she didn't want to write a trace anymore that was fine with me.

Ms. March found me and she said: Logan, Mr. Jeffries said you didn't show up yesterday for the tree construction.

Me: I went to the stage and no one was there.

Ms. March: Oh, yes. I'm sorry about the mix-up. A couple of other people got confused also. The tree making is located in the art room. Mr. Jeffries is heading it up. I'm sorry I wasn't clear about that yesterday.

Me: Mmmphh [or something like that].

Ms. March: You'll go there after practice, won't you? They really need bodies, Logan.

Me: Okay.

Ms. March: I told Mr. Jeffries he could rely on you. He can, can't he, Logan?

Me: Yeah, okay.

I didn't know what else to say.

I mean, what could I say when she just asks me like that?

So I went.

After my fight with Bruce and the shovel, Scouts was worse than anything.

Jack was still so mad it was hard for him to even look at me.

But he told me he wouldn't tell anyone. Not even Patsy, and he made Bruce promise too. This was because of Dad and he felt bad for him and he didn't think he deserved the crap he'd heard had happened to Dad and Mom and our family because of me.

In Jack and Patsy's kitchen right after the fight with him and Bruce:

Jack: I was giving you the benefit of the doubt but you've proven your reputation, Logan.

Me:

Jack: I really can't believe this.

Me:

Bruce: He's such a jerk, Dad. He totally attacked me for no reason. He's psycho.

He's really psycho.

Jack: Okay, okay, Bruce. I'll deal with this. You go get cleaned up and don't tell your mother about this.

Bruce: What? Why not?

Jack: Because I say so.

Bruce: But?.?.?.

Jack: Are you still talking? Go get cleaned up and we'll go shopping for that stuff you wanted after all the boys finish their fires.

Bruce gave me a look that I can't say and then he left.

Then Jack in my face.

Jack: This is because I like your dad. If you ever touch my kid again?.?.?.? if you ever touch anyone in this neighborhood, I'll know. I know about you and I'll know. I want you at Scouts on time, every time, and don't make one misstep or else. One misstep?.?.?.? I'm warning you.

Now, go home, Logan.

*

When I finally went back to Dr. Benson for my second appointment, I was ready.

Mom and Dad at first said I didn't have to go and I said: Good.

Then, later, I heard Mom crying: It's my fault. I was so manipulative. We should've told him what it was all about.

Dad: Yeah, we should've told him, Sil. But we didn't know how to handle it.

And my mom was sort of sobbing. That's when I went into their room.

They both stopped talking. Ugghh.

Me: Okay, what now?

Dad: I'm sorry, Logan. I'm sorry about everything.

My mom was trying to pull it together. She looked pretty bad – I'm not used to seeing her like that.

I went over and sort of hugged her.

Me: It's okay, Mom.

Mom: Oh, Logan, it's not okay. It's not okay. We keep messing up.

And she was sobbing again, this time into the shoulder of my sweater, and it was really weird.

She was shaking and I didn't know what to do and Dad was just sitting in his chair looking at his hands.

Finally Mom went into the bathroom to wipe up her mascara.

Me: What does she mean, keep messing up?

Dad: She means that we didn't know how to protect you back on Mulholland and we thought Judge would be a better place for you. A place you could maybe restart.

Me:

Mom came back and sat on the bed. I was still standing there. Mom was so upset I wondered if it would hurt the baby. I think I read about that somewhere.

Dad: But, Logan, it's pretty obvious it's not going to go away. That's why we found Dr. Benson. He's really good and some friends recommended him very highly. We just thought it would be a good idea?.?.?.

Mom: We thought it would help if you talked about it. You never talk about it. You always just sit in that room.

Me:

Mom: And I should have told you where we were going but lately I never know what you're going to do. I don't know what's going on in your head. You barely talk about anything anymore. I don't know how to help you. I don't.

She was rambling and then crying again.

Dad: Silvia. It's okay.

Mom: No, it's not. It's not.

That's when she left the room and went I don't know where.

I was sick of being in the middle of everything.

Me: Dad, I'm fine.

Dad: I know you are. You are. You're handling everything a lot better than I would if I were in your situation. But do you think you could at least talk to this guy – a couple times? That would really help your mother, and I think it could maybe even help you.

84

I told him I would.

I told him I'd do whatever so that everyone could stop worrying about me.

And he said thanks: It was weird to have him say thanks how he did.

So the next time I went to Dr. Benson, I was ready.

Dr. Benson: So, Logan, how are you feeling?

Me: Fine.

Dr. Benson: I'm sorry about last time. I guess it would've been better had you known what you were getting into.

Me: Yes.

Dr. Benson: Do you feel better now?

Me: Yes.

Dr. Benson: Do you know why you're here?

Me: Yes.

Dr. Benson: Do you want to tell me?

Me: Not really.

Dr. Benson: Why not?

Me: Because you already know.

Dr. Benson: Okay, that's fair. Well, why don't you tell me a little about yourself? You're in junior high, right?

Me: Yes.

Dr. Benson: Why don't you tell me a little about that?

Me: It's fine.

Dr. Benson: So you like it?

Me: It's okay.

Dr. Benson: Let's talk about okay. What does okay feel like?

Me:

Dr. Benson: Do you understand what I'm asking?

Me: Not really.

Dr. Benson: Okay, I'm asking you to think about what you generally feel like when you go to school. You say okay. But I don't get what okay means. Does okay mean you don't dread going? Does it mean you like going? Does it mean you prefer it over other things?

Me: I don't know.

That's pretty much how the whole "session" went. I knew what he was trying to do and I knew it wouldn't work. I'd cooperate however I wanted to and that's it.

Dr. Benson didn't get anything out of me.

Nothing.

Bruce found a weight-loss shake in my bag.

So Scouts was worse and Bruce and Toby and Luke laughed all the time because I'm crapstock and a molester, they said.

But I still went on time, every time.

Not one misstep.

So that Dad and Mom wouldn't know.

Every time I went I'd just try not to talk or get in anyone's way.

The other guys didn't seem to hate me like Bruce and his followers did, but they didn't seem to like me much either.

I mean, they didn't talk to me and they were probably scared of me.

So that's why when Jack brought up the Klondike Derby, I knew I had to find a way out. I also knew it would be next to impossible to get out of it because it was required: Jack made a big deal about it, and my dad had legendary stories about his Klondike Derby days.

But I tried.

I tried and I tried.

But I didn't try hard enough.

Sometimes I wish I could erase everything that happened that night with Zyler.

I'd just go home after dinner and not to Zyler's house.

Maybe I'd call him and he'd come over.

If we'd been at my house it wouldn't have happened.

Nothing would have happened.

*

One time I asked Zyler how come he didn't turn his dad in or any-thing.

He shrugged and kept shooting cans.

I didn't know if I should ask again but then

He said: You don't get it.

Me: What do you mean?

Zyler: Where would I go if Dad was gone?

Me:

Zyler: Sometimes you don't get anything.

Me:

Zyler: Besides, it never works.

Me: You mean you've tried?

Zyler: I haven't. But people have.

Me: Who?

Zyler: People.

He was quiet and then he shot a can. I sat there and then

Zyler: The worst one was Mrs. Magelby.

Me: Mrs. Magelby?

Mrs. Magelby was our fifth grade teacher and I couldn't believe she of all people would try to rat out Zyler's dad.

Me: Why was it the worst? What happened?

Zyler: I came to school and I guess I had a black eye or a big lip or something and she asked me about it and I said that I had fallen down or hit the door or something. And she got all mad and said she wouldn't let it happen again. It'd gone on long enough.

He shot another can.

Me: So?

I still couldn't imagine it. I mean, I could see her getting all concerned because she was our best teacher in elementary. Really young and pretty and really nice, but not tough or anything. Not anyone to take on Zyler's dad.

Zyler:

Me: So? What did she do? Did she call Child Services or anything?

Mom was always saying Child Services would have Zyler's dad's head or something.

Zyler: No Child Services – she went straight to the source.

He missed a can.

Me: What do you mean?

Zyler: She went to see my dad right after school.

I almost choked on the candy I was chewing. We were in the field by the lake that's out past the freeway, and like usual, he was shooting and I was watching – no guns, says Mom.

Me: What happened?

Zyler: Nothing.

Me: What do you mean?

Zyler:

Me: What happened?

Zyler: I don't know. I know she came over. I know I had to go to my room. I know I heard my dad's voice real loud. I know she never called anyone.

Me: Wow.

Zyler: Shut up.

Me: What was that for?

Zyler: Sorry.

Me: It's okay.

And that was it.

My parents were always really nice to Zyler and let him sleep over.

He could even eat whatever he wanted even though we didn't have good food and Mom was usually anal about snacks and stuff, but not when Zyler was around.

She said we just had to love him.

I know she'd talked to Dad about letting him live with us or doing something.

But Dad said we couldn't and he wasn't their son or anything and we didn't know all the circumstances and being a single parent was hard.

But see, they didn't know what really went on and I barely did and Zyler didn't want anyone to know.

Zyler: Don't tell anyone about my dad or anything.

Me: Why?

Zyler: Just don't.

Me: Okay. But it's pretty obvious.

Zyler: People need to mind their own business or else it could get not good, get it?
Me: Yeah.
But I didn't really get it.
Zyler: Promise me you won't say anything about my dad or anything.
Me: Okay.

Dr. Benson?.?.?.
He's actually not that bad.
He hates snow camping and he was in the school band.
He's okay.

After play practice I didn't wait for anyone like Laurel or the other ones who signed up for set making.
I just walked straight to the art room in C wing because I knew if I didn't go straight I'd never go again, and I told Ms. March I would.
Mr. Jeffries was there. I have him for fifth period: Art 1.
He went: Ahh, Mr. Paloney. I'm so glad you're here. We missed you yesterday.

Me: Thanks [It was all I could think of to say: Thanks].

Mr. Jeffries: Well, since you're the first one, why don't you help me get started on the trunk.

Mr. Jeffries was a pretty cool guy with a mustache and jeans instead of ties like a lot of other teachers. Plus, he thought I was good at things like collages and he said my pencil drawing of my tennis shoe was: Right on.

I said okay and I watched him showing us how to hammer the plywood together.

As he was talking, people – not very many, but some – started com-ing in.

They all seemed to know where to go, what to do.

Laurel came in semi-last and she went straight to where they were making leaves.

She didn't look at me.

There hadn't been any notes because I didn't ever write back and I knew she probably hated me.

But then I did something.

I had to use a staple gun and there was one over by the leaves.

Me: Does anyone know where a staple gun is?

I knew it was by her, but I said it anyway.

Laurel: It's right here.

And she handed it to me.

When I took it she didn't let it go right away. That made me look at her. She looked back and sort of smiled.

And then she let go.

I was confused but I guess sort of relieved.
I decided to find out more about Laurel.

Stuff I know from just watching:
She got a C on her pre-algebra test about balancing the equation. I got a B+.
She has a locker in D wing.
Stuff I know from Lael, who lives on her street:
She lives on Richter Street.
She has maybe one or two brothers and sisters and her parents are normal.
Her mom used to be an actress and everyone knows it because she was in community shows and in the parade.
Laurel also won the spelling bee in sixth grade and went all the way to regionals – Lael was mad about that.
Oh, and Lael thinks she's crazy.

I sort of tried to tell Jack I didn't want to go on the Klondike Derby.
It took me a long time to tell him because I didn't know what to say and he hated me anyway.
WUSS.

That's what I am.

CRAPSTOCK.

Me at one of our preparatory pack meetings: Jack?

Jack:

He was helping some kid make a first-aid kit.

Me: Jack?

Jack: What, Paloney?

Me: Can I talk to you?

Jack: Does it look like you can talk to me?

Me:

I didn't really get what that meant.

Jack: Talk to me later.

That was the first attempt.

The Klondike Derby is like this: You have to sleep in a snow cave and you have to make the cave yourself.

Dad took me to the Camping Outfitters to get a hiking snow shovel that's small and you can fold up, some better boots, a down coat, a bivvy sack for my sleeping bag, a pair of good gloves and mittens to go on top, a little stove and gas just in case, and a bunch of hand and feet warmers.

We were going one night.

Dad said: I can't tell you how exhilarating this trip is going to be for you. There's nothing like the winter night air. Or the vigorous physical labor of building your own shelter or the warmth that comes from inside your own creation. It's pure bliss.

Me: Uh-huh.

Dad: Did Jack take you all out and show you different methods of building your cave? Because there are lots of ways to do it.

Me: He's going to next time.

Dad: I sure wish I could go. I really do, Logan. It would be a great adventure.

Me: Yeah.

Jack had invited Dad and I had prayed he would say yes but he couldn't. He had a business trip that very weekend and he couldn't change it.

No way.

So no Dad.

Just me, Jack, Bruce, Toby, and three other guys.

At least Luke wasn't going.

He didn't get good enough grades. Good excuse.

The day before the Derby, Jack came over to pick up my stuff.

He was loading his truck early so we could get up there with daylight.

It was, I guess, a really long drive.

Dad: Jack, this is really just great.

Jack:

Dad: I'm so glad Logan is getting this chance.

Jack: Yeah, Tom. It's going to be great for all the boys.

There was definite irritation in his voice and I didn't want him to say anything to Dad but I knew he might.

I mean, he said he wouldn't but he might.

I was just sitting on the stairs watching my dad take things out.

He gave Jack some extra stuff in case people forgot their pad or a shovel or whatever.

Dad: Is there anything I can do? I'm so disappointed I can't go.

Jack looked at him and then he looked at me. Then he took Dad by the arm and they went outside.

Crapstock.

I went down into my room.

It wasn't my fault.

I didn't know what to do.

I don't think it was my fault.

Was it?

I feel so bad about Cami and I was so sorry too.

I wonder if she still hates flies or what she does.

Sometimes I still want to call her and tell her so much stuff but especially that I didn't mean to not do anything and that I'm sorry too.

*

When Bruce found that weight-loss shake in my bag *that* was pretty much my fault.

I mean, I'd left my bag open in science sort of and we were doing a lab and it was the first and only time I'd taken one to school.

Usually I just drink them down in my room and Mom thinks Dad's drinking them, but I heard Dad say he thinks they taste like chalk, but I had lost three pounds so I decided to have one for lunch and so I put it in my bag under my books and forgot about it.

In science we were dissecting squid.

Mrs. Bernam: Everyone get with your lab partners. And one of you retrieve a tray from the back cupboards.

I was with this kid Eddie and he doesn't talk or do anything so I just went to get the tray.

That's when I guess Bruce took it.

I got back and I didn't notice anything but Eddie was sort of giving me a look – like nodding at something.

He was nodding at them.

Taking sips.

Bruce: Oh, oh, this is so good. I love these shakes. They make my body lean and smooth.

Umm.

Toby: Maybe with these shakes I can lose my fat ass and I can get girls to touch me.

Yeesssss.

People were laughing and Mrs. Bernam was out of it helping someone unwrap their squid. Teachers are useless.

Bruce: Oh, I'm sorry, Logan. Did you need this today? Does your fat ass need it? Because we thought you've been looking so right lately that we'd like a try.

Me:

Bruce: It seems he doesn't mind if we drink up this refreshing treat.

He passed the drink around.

By then Mrs. Bernam was scanning the room.

Bruce and his boys were busy pulling on gloves and pulling on squid tentacles.

Eddie was quiet and I was crapstock.

It didn't really matter.

I saw Laurel in the hall.

It was between sixth and seventh.

She handed me the empty weight-loss can and handed me another note.

Logan —
Too far Edna, we wander afoot.
Laurel

Later that day Laurel said something to me and it was this: Good job with your stunt.

It was at play rehearsal.

I think it was the second time we had ever sort of talked.

She said it because at one point all the Lost Boys have to wrestle with the pirates.

And me and this one kid, who is the pirate I fight, we do this fake tackle that we made up and we even practice it on the side when we don't have anything to do or when we're not in the scenes or anything.

So when we did it in front for the first time I guess it looked really cool and really real. Even Ms. March thought so and she might have us be right in the front for the whole fighting scene because we made it up ourselves.

The pirate's name is Melvin and he's a ninth grader and he thinks he can get a scholarship to Duke through his fencing.

He's cool to talk to.

And Laurel said: Good job with your stunt.

I said: Thanks.

She said:

I said: Umm.

And I didn't know if I should say anything about the can.

I said: Thanks for the can.

She said: I know.

And that was it.

I am in the front for the fight scene for sure now and I've lost two more pounds.

Mom knows about the shakes but she said it's okay and she'll get me more.

At school Bruce said: You got any more shakes in there? It was really, really good.

Girls like Carmen and Vanessa and Mallory laughed.

Me:

Bruce: Come on, Logan. Let us have another one. We loved it.

One of the girls: Please, Logan.

Another one: Pretty please?

Me:

Bruce: In fact, if you give us one of your drinks, I'm sure Mallory will make out with you, won't you, Mal?

One of the girls with the blond hair: Shut up, Bruce.

Bruce: Just say you'll make him happy, Mal.

Mallory: Shut up.

Bruce: What's your problem?

Another of the girls: Leave Mal alone.

Me:

And then I walked away because it was almost like they forgot I was there.

I was glad.

I drank my shake in the bathroom.

Dad bought an elliptical machine.

He got it at Gart Sports because he went there with Mom and came back with the minivan all loaded up.

They honked and when we came out Dad was opening the back hatch and Mom was sort of jumping up and down.

She said: I'm so excited. Look what your father bought.

And Dad looked sort of mad.

Mack: Wow, cool. It's an elliptical.

Ryan: Those things are expensive.

Mack: Are you still going to get the new basketball standard?

Dad didn't answer. He was trying to get it out of the back and we were all staring.

Mom: Go help your father, boys. Oh, it's going to be so great.

We put it in the family room. In the corner so if you used it you could watch TV.

Dad used it twice.

I use it sometimes.

After everyone is asleep, because it's hard to get the rhythm right and I look stupid.

But it's pretty good.

Yesterday I went outside when Mack and Ryan were shooting and I sat on the grass.

Ryan: Want to play?

Me: That's okay.

Mack: Come on, barf bag. Let's play horse. We haven't played forever.

And it was true, we hadn't.

So I said okay and then I played.

I also told them about palindromes and this one: Butt raft fart tub.

They couldn't believe it and it was so funny and we were laughing so hard.

Dr. Benson asks me a lot of questions.

Mostly about Zyler now.

Dr. Benson: Well, have you tried to contact him?

Me: No.

Dr. Benson: Why not?

Me: I don't know. I don't think I can.

Dr. Benson: I don't see why you couldn't.

Me: I don't even know where they put him.

Dr. Benson: Well, I'm sure we could find out.

Me: I don't know.

Dr. Benson: You don't know what?

Me: I don't know if it's a good idea to go around looking for him.

Dr. Benson: I don't understand what you mean.

Me:

Dr. Benson:

Me:

Dr. Benson: Do you want to talk about it?

Me: I don't know.

Dr. Benson: Okay. Okay, let's see. So you haven't contacted him. You don't know where he is and you don't know if you want to contact him.

Me: My parents are always asking me this but I don't know. I mean, I want to contact him or whatever but I don't know if it'd be a good idea.

Dr. Benson: A good idea because he might get in trouble or something?

Me: Would he?

Dr. Benson: I seriously doubt it.

Me: Oh.

Dr. Benson: Or maybe you're scared to talk to him.

Me:

Dr. Benson: Is that it?

Me:

Dr. Benson: Logan?

Me: No. I'm not scared. I don't feel like talking about this.

Dr. Benson: Okay.

Logan
TEN ANIMALS IN A NET
Laurel
*actually three. get it?

I didn't get it.

Sometimes Laurel is kind of weird.

When we were putting the leaves on the branches for the Lost
Boys tree, Laurel whispered to me: Did you get it?

Me:

Laurel: Well?

Me: I don't know.

Laurel: Is it true?

Me: What?

Laurel: You know.

I kept nailing things in and tried to think. I didn't know what she was talking about all the way.

Laurel: Heeeeeyyyyy.

And she poked me.

I shook my head.

People were looking at us.

She said: Meet me by D wing, by the bushes, after we're done.

Me:

I met Laurel out there.

At D wing.

We stopped working on the tree when Mr. Jeffries said: Okay, that's it for today. Good job, you guys.

And then I got my backpack and when I looked up Laurel was gone.

I thought maybe she forgot about D wing because she left so fast, so I was just going to call my mom for a ride.

But then I thought I'd just see.

I went down B wing and outside into the quad.

D wing isn't attached to the school.

It's its own building. And it's sort of called skater wing because that's where the skaters hang out and everything.

But not two and a half hours after school.

And Laurel wasn't there. No one was and the door was locked.

I guess she forgot and I was glad because I didn't really want to talk to her.

At least not about what I think she wanted to talk about.

But then this: Hey?.?.?.

She was whispering, but really loud, and it was coming from behind the bushes on the west side.

Again: Logan, hey?.?.?.

Me: Is that you?

Laurel: Shhhhhhhhhhhhhhhhhhhh. Come over here. We don't want anyone to see us.

I went over to the general area and started to say: Where are you?—

But she grabbed my arm and pulled me to this little area that was sort of like a cave behind the bushes – kind of like me and Zyler's spot but not really.

Laurel: Shhhh. Don't you know how to be quiet?

It was a strange question for a lot of reasons: #1. I'm always quiet and my dad says too quiet. I need to learn to speak up. And #2. What was I supposed to say? Was I supposed to answer it?

Me:

Laurel: Sit down against the wall so no one will see us.

She shoved her brown hair behind her ears and she looked sort of freaky because her pirate makeup was all smeared. She had some on her hand so I think she accidentally messed it up.

And I probably knew why she didn't want anyone to see us but it sort of made me feel sort of bad.

Laurel: What took you so long?

Me: Uhhhhhh.

Laurel: Shhh. We have to whisper.

Me: Why?

Laurel: So no one will know, duh. I said it like fifty times.

Me:

Laurel: Is something wrong with you?

Again I was confused.

Me: No.

Laurel: Then what's your problem?

Me: Why do we have to hide? It's two and a half hours after school.

Laurel: I'm not supposed to be talking to you. And you're not supposed to be talking to me. Not any girls.

Me:

Laurel: I know, duh. I know all about everything, duh.

Me: What are you talking about?

Laurel: Your past.

Me: What?

Laurel: That's why I want to talk to you. I don't really believe those dorkfaceoffs but they said they'd be watching and they said you were on court restraint order probation and you weren't supposed to be talking to girls and they were going to be watching both you and me because they think we're friends. Because of the notes, you know. By the way, did you get what I meant with the last few notes? The carton and the wander afoot and the animals??It was code: Keep quiet and we'll rendezvous and talk about getting those animals in a net.

Me:

Laurel: Like Bruce and all those guys are animals and we need to stop them.

Me:

I didn't know what to say.

Laurel: And anyway, so do you have one?

Me: I don't have a net.

Laurel: No. We're not really going to get them in a net, duh. I just mean we need to get back at them. That's what I meant.

Me:

Laurel: So? Is it true? Do you have one?

Me: What?

Laurel: A court restraint order probation or whatever.

Me: No.

Laurel: I didn't think so but anyway, I just thought we should rendezvous and talk it out.

I had to think, but she just kept talking.

She talked about Bruce and Luke and Toby and she said: Did you know in elementary Bruce won the school art contest every time?

Me:

Laurel: He did and it was because his mom did it or hired someone to do it. You could tell. You could so tell. Once he turned in this painting that was all dots – Pointillism is what my mom said it was. The whole thing was a bunch of dots that made up this scene of a barn and a sunset.

She stopped and looked at me. I could tell she wanted a reaction.

Me: Really?

Laurel: Yeah! Can you believe it? And there was no way because in class all he ever drew were like these stupid tanks and stuff – plus, they didn't even look real. My mom was going to complain because she's on the school board and she thought it was unfair, but then she didn't because there was this big issue with the funds and Mom was the spokesman for that and she had to defend her friend Peggy who was also on the school board but she's not anymore. But Mom didn't feel like she could get into the middle of anything right then, plus, it would look like she was doing it just because I got second prize with my drawing of an ostrich running really fast through a city like New York. It was symbolic. Did you know ostriches can run, like, forty or fifty miles an hour?

Me: Yeah, and they also can't fly.

I knew that because I did my third grade report on the ostrich. It was kind of cool she knew about them. They have the best eggs too – they are huge and the mom ostriches bury them.

Laurel: I know. So anyway, Mom didn't want to be one of *those* kind of moms so we just let it go.

Me:

Then she just kept talking.

She said how Bruce and those guys were saying how I was a danger to girls and that was why I was so quiet and I never talked to girls, and I was one of the silent sick types and they'd seen me looking at her and even though they didn't like her (like she cared), they felt a duty and she should beware because if she got linked up with me it would either hurt her physically because of what I had done and what I was probably going to do again or hurt her socially (ha), like worse off than she already was and she was on thin ice (especially since last year she sent a note around about how Bruce had wet his pants five times in third grade), and she said she didn't really care what they said, but she did want to know the truth and what she was up against and how maybe we could get them back, but we couldn't until she knew what she was dealing with.

It was more than any girl had ever said to me in my whole life, not including family and my mom's best friend, Nora, and Nora talks a lot.

Me:

Laurel: Just think about what I've said and we'll meet here again tomorrow. We've been here too long anyway. Wait eight minutes after I leave to leave.

And then she was gone.

I left eight minutes after she did.

*

I think Laurel is not what I thought.

I'm not sure if I should like her or not.

Sometimes I think she likes me and sometimes I think she thinks I'm stupid.

I don't know.

Most things and people are not what I thought.

Mom and Dad are excited about the play.

Mom is really pregnant now and so she has to sit a lot.

She had Dad rent every *Peter Pan* video there was at Blockbuster so she could see what Lost Boys do.

I already told her: Lost Boys are the ones who get lost. So they follow Peter Pan around and do whatever they want and that's all.

But she wanted to see for herself, so we all had to watch four *Peter Pan* videos.

Mack and Ryan didn't last one movie.

They had practice anyway.

Dad had work.

But Mom and I saw them all and had pretzels.

It was actually sort of cool to see the part I was doing and them fighting the pirates.

I still think the move I do in the fight scene is the coolest: even more than the movies.

111

The Klondike Derby.

We had to meet at Jack's at 6:30 a.m.

In his Suburban.

And the seats went like this:

Driver: Jack

Passenger seat: Richard (the other leader)

Middle bench: Bruce, Taylor, Toby

Back bench: Me, Chris, Sam

That was good.

Lucky.

I thought.

Because I didn't have to sit by Bruce.

I was directly behind him but not next to him, and he had to twist all the way around to see me or anything.

But actually one thing was bad because Jack couldn't see clear back to the back so good and he definitely couldn't hear.

Bruce: Chris and Sam?.?.?.?I'd watch it. You're sitting by a loser crapstock molester.

This was just before we stopped for gas and just after I thought I was safe because they hadn't said anything yet and it seemed like everyone was just going to sleep and maybe I'd be okay.

No.

Chris and Sam just sort of laughed.

Bruce: I'm serious. The guy is a disease, aren'tcha, crapstock?

I looked out the window.

Toby and Taylor were twisted around looking at me too.

Jack: Everything okay back there?

Bruce: Yeah, Dad. We're just playing a game.

Jack: No messing around, Bruce. I'm serious. Turn around.

Bruce: Okay, Dad. Sheesh.

They all turned forward and I still looked out the window.

Jack started talking to Richard after a while and then Bruce turned on the radio from the backseat.

It was a nice Suburban.

Bruce and the rest twisted again.

Bruce: Okay, you guys. I have a game for real. We're going to play the alphabet game. Each of us has to go in order and think of a good new name for crapstock here.

I'll go first. A—Assface

I bit my lip. I hated him. I hated him.

Toby: B—Buttknockers

Why did we have to move to Judge?

Taylor:

Bruce: Don't wuss out, Taylor.

Taylor: C?.?.?.?Crapstock?

Bruce: We'll let that suffice for now because you're amateur. Chris?

I started to sweat.

Chris: D—Dorkapokia.

Bruce: Needs work. Try harder next letter.

He looked at Sam.

Sam was the nicest to me the whole time in Scouts.

He never really did anything to me or joined in and one time, he even walked home with me. That was because Bruce and his friends were at a birthday party so they weren't at Scouts or anything.

That was a good day.

Bruce: Come on, Sam. You can do it.

Sam:

Bruce: Are my suspicions right? Are you and crapstocky in love? Ohmigosh, you guys, it's a regular romance.

I was still looking out the window trying not to smash him. Trying not to smash his face.

Sam: E—eats-his-mom's-poo-for-breakfast?

They all laughed.

Bruce: All right, crapstock. It's your turn. Now's your chance to rename yourself.

Me:

I was glued to the glass. Hands clenched.

Bruce: Come on, crappy. You have the best letter too. F. What's it going to be, or do you want me to help you out?

Me:

Bruce: If you don't come up with a name fast, I already have one, perfect. I'll give you a few more seconds.

Toby: Bruce, crapstock looks a bit upset. Should we leave him alone a bit to think and cool down? Maybe he can't take the pressure.

Bruce: That's a very charitable thought, my friend. Very

charitable, indeed. I was almost thinking the same thing. But then I think our fellow Scouts would be disappointed if we let him off the hook. What do you think, boys?

No one said anything and then

Chris: Make him do it.

Taylor: Yeah. We had to.

Bruce: Shoot, crapstock. Looks like you better say something fast or you're going to get it.

And he shoved my face into the glass.

Hard.

That's when I flipped – again.

For the second time in front of Jack.

I lunged over the seat.

Grabbing at Bruce's face.

Scratching him and shoving and I guess pushing him into Jack's seat.

Jack swerved.

We all swerved.

He went off the road.

He was screaming, swearing.

And that was just the beginning.

*

The next time I met with Dr. Benson he just kept asking about Zyler.

Dr. Benson: What would you say to him if you had a chance?

Me: I don't know.

Dr. Benson: I don't believe that.

Me:

Dr. Benson: Just try, Logan. What do you want to tell him?

Me: I'm sorry, I guess. I don't know.

Dr. Benson: Sorry for what?

Me: Sorry for leaving him. And sorry for not helping.

Dr. Benson: When?

Me: I don't know.

Dr. Benson: Push harder, Logan. You're sorry for leaving him when?

Me: When it happened, I guess. And other times.

Dr. Benson: What other times?

Me: I don't know.

Dr. Benson:

Me: I guess when I knew what his dad was like. And when I found out.

Dr. Benson: What does that mean, Logan? Found out what?

Me:

Dr. Benson:

Me: I don't want to talk about it.

Dr. Benson: Why not?

Me:

Dr. Benson: Logan?

Me: Because it wasn't my fault.

And it wasn't.

Dr. Benson: I'm not saying it was. You know that.

Me: Yeah.

Dr. Benson:

Me:

Dr. Benson:

Me:

Dr. Benson:

Me:

Dr. Benson: I called his social worker.

Me:

Me Me Me Me Me Me Me Me Me Me Me Me Me Me Me Me
Me Me Me Me Me Me:

Dr. Benson: I know where he is and we might be able to contact
him soon.

That's all.

I met Laurel the next day in the bushes.

It feels funny to say that.

In the bushes.

When I got there she was already sitting against the wall eating

117

Disney Princess Fruit Snacks.

Laurel: You're late.

She ate a green princess.

And I was late because Mr. Jeffries wanted me to stay even later after the other guys to help him get supports in the tree.

Me:

Laurel: Why do you do that?

Me: Do what?

Laurel: Nothing.

Nothing? I didn't know what she meant.

Me:

Laurel: See?

Me: What?

Laurel: Why do you always just sit there? Why don't you talk?

Me:

I was trying to get what she was saying. It didn't matter.

But right then instead of her saying something else we heard talking. Loud talking and it wasn't anyone I knew but Laurel said: Hit the dirt!

She sort of yelled-whispered it and shoved my head toward my legs. It hurt.

Girls like Carmen and Vanessa and Mallory.

Them: I hate that! Are you serious? No way. Yep. Really? Who said? I know.

And then they were gone.

Me: They're gone.

Laurel: I don't care.

And she was picking at her toes.

Laurel: Hey, do you like corn dogs?

Me: Uhhh, I guess.

Laurel: Well, I do. I do so much. And they used to have them in elementary on Tuesdays but they never have them here. Have you noticed that?

I wasn't quite sure what to do because she was staring right at me so I said:

And then she said: Well?

Me: What?

Laurel: Anyway, I think you're cool. Better than those dorks and not what they say and one day I'm going to work at the Corn Dog Factory.

And then she was looking even harder at me. I think the dorks were supposed to be girls like Carmen and Vanessa and Mallory.

Me:

Laurel: Do you know the Corn Dog Factory?

Of course I knew the Corn Dog Factory. There was one at both the Cherry Creek Mall and the Park Meadows Mall. It's the one where the workers have to wear tall red-yellow-and-white-striped hats that look like popcorn buckets, and then matching shirts and shorts.

Me: Yeah.

Laurel: Do you think it'd be dumb to work there?

Me: No.

Laurel: I don't either. I think it would be so cool. Free corn dogs all day and fresh lemonade too. If you wanted, I could probably get you a discount.

Me:

Laurel:

Me: Okay.

Then she said she had to go and then: Be back here tomorrow.

Me: Okay.

But she was too loud and moving her stuff and gone.

When we finally drove into the national park I was glad.

I was sitting in front.

Mouth shut.

No moving.

Even at pit stops.

Jack: Okay, guys. We're here!

And everyone started getting out.

I didn't really know what to do because I wasn't supposed to move, so I just sat there.

And they were all outside getting their stuff out of the back.

Jack: Paloney, where the hell are you?

Me:

I just sort of got out and my stuff was in the snow outside the back of the Suburban.

Everyone else was already walking up the trail.

I tried to get all my stuff together but then

Me: Hey, Jack!

I yelled it because they were all talking.

Jack:

Me: Jack!

Really loud.

Me: Where's my sleeping bag?!

They all kept walking.

So I didn't have a sleeping bag for the Klondike Derby and I
know Dad even gave Jack extras.

When I finally caught up to them

Jack: Okay, boys. We'll set up right over there.

He pointed to a clearing.

Everyone sort of grumbled or said stuff and then Jack: Let's
start shoveling.

Me when everyone was doing other things: Jack?

Jack:

Me:

I decided not to bring up the sleeping bag for a while.

So I helped build the snow caves and I didn't talk to anyone.

And no one talked to me.

Jack and Richard reminded us how to build and then said: You guys are on your own.

First you make a huge mound of snow.

Huge.

And then you dig it out.

It took us hours.

Lots of hours, and even though I thought they were doing it a stupid way – they weren't even thinking about the pressure of the snow on the roof and it kept falling in so we'd have to start over and Bruce would yell and Jack wouldn't help us because it was for our merit badge – I didn't say anything.

By the time we were done it was really dark and really cold.

Jack: We've got beans and hot dogs and hot chocolate over here.

He and Richard had a fire going.

I had to sit the farthest from the fire because there wasn't that much room.

I didn't care.

Later that night.

Jack: I know we brought your bag, Paloney. Maybe one of the other boys picked it up.

Me:

Jack: What do you want me to do about it?

And he was now almost in my face with his flashlight and I wished he wouldn't be so loud.

Jack: I'm sick of your stunts, Logan. Go to sleep.

I wanted to ask him about the extra stuff my dad had given him and how come he didn't have that stuff.

But I didn't ask.

Me:

And so he walked away.

Over to his snow cave.

Me standing there.

Looking at his cave and then over at our cave.

It was ten at night.

And the moon had finally come out from behind the clouds.

Lighter.

Almost bright off the snow and the trees' shadows.

I closed my eyes and wasn't with Jack and any of those guys.

Just me and Zyler.

Hanging out.

Like that one night when it was so snowy and we rode our bikes in the blizzard.

Down the middle of the road because there were no cars anywhere.

We didn't even have coats on but it didn't feel cold.

And Zyler was yelling things like: Santa Claus is dead! We own you all!

I was laughing. And riding around. And wasn't even scared about what Mom would say.

The snow landing on my tongue.

On my cheeks.

On my bare arms.

In circles and circles and circles.

And I was not here. Not here. Not HERE. Not here.

I don't know how long I stood there in the snow

With the moon

And Zyler

And my bike

But then

Bruce: Hey, fairy, bring your flashlight back!

Dad told me that if you had the right equipment, snow mountaineering was the most exhilarating blah blah ever.

But without the right equipment, hypothermia would start and even the strongest men could die.

I weigh 131 pounds and it's mostly fat.

Not strong.

I had a lot of clothes on and plus some really good boots and gloves.

I walked over to the Scout cave.

It was silent, but then whispers.

I started to crawl in.

It smelled worse than Mack and Ryan farting.

Too many guys.

So I was starting to crawl in when Bruce said: I don't think so.

Me:

I was just kneeling there and he said: I don't think so.

Me: What?

Him: It's not safe.

Me:

Toby: Yeah, we don't want to get attacked or anything while we sleep. Go dig your own cave.

And then he threw a shovel at me.

It wasn't a big shovel or anything like that.

Just a small red one you use for snow.

But it still hurt.

Kind of.

And all the guys were laughing and I didn't care.

I didn't care except it sort of hurt.

Bruce: Well, guys, maybe we should let him stay in here. It's really quite cold out.

Me:

I didn't want to be out there alone and my face hurt and I was cold.

Them: Laughing.

Me:

Bruce: I guess we could let you. But why don't you try to convince us first. Feed us some of your crap that you fed your parents about how you were innocent.

Me:

Chris: Innocent about what?

Me:

Bruce: Oh yeah. My mom said he hurt this girl real bad. Probably did worse stuff but the girl didn't say. She won't talk.

Chris: Really?

Me:

Bruce:

Me:

Bruce: It doesn't matter. He has a court restraint on him and he probably can't ever get a job in his life. Dad said that.

The guys were staring at me.

I stared back.

Bruce: I'm tired. Aren't you guys tired?

Them:

Bruce: We have to get up early tomorrow.

And it was true.

We had the stupid Klondike sled competition and other stuff starting at seven the next day.

They all sort of got into their sleeping bags and they were turning out their flashlights when I saw this: My sleeping bag.

Bruce: Sorry, Logan, we were just kidding. You can sleep in here.

My sleeping bag, over by the far snow wall – all laid out.

I didn't know who had my sleeping bag and who set it up, but at that point I didn't care.

Jack probably made them give it to me.

If I died he could get sued.

It smelled seriously sick in the cave.

But I didn't say anything.

I crawled over and put my pack down.

The sleeping bag really was perfectly laid out.

So I slid in and that's when

I

Realized.

Them: hahahahahahahahahahahahahahahahahahahahahahaha
hahahahahahahahahahahahahahahahahahahahahahahahahahahah
ahahahahahaha hahahahahahahahahahahahahahahahaha

Bruce: You really are crapstock, Paloney.

It was all over.

I was all over in it.

I couldn't breathe.

I

Couldn't

Breathe.

What to do?

I crawled back out.

Them: Oh, sick. SICK! You stink, man. That is disgusting. Someone light a match.

And on and on and on.

Outside I tried to get some of it off in the snow but it was really all over.

My sleeping bag came flying out of the snow cave.

I tried not to cry.

Me: I'm not going to cry. I'm not going to cry.

But then I did.

I tried to wake Jack up.

I tried to tell him what they did.

I sort of yelled in his cave: Jack?

The cave:

Me: Jack.

The cave:

And then me louder: Jack!

His head out the hole: What are you doing?! Go to sleep.

And then I said what had happened. I was crying and sort of slobbering and shaking I was so cold from trying to get it off with snow.

And Jack did this: Sort of laugh.

He sort of laughed and said: Go to sleep.

And the head was gone.

*

This is how the fight between my dad and Jack happened.

After the big blowout bang down crap crap crap crap crap double crap Derby I refused to go to SCOUTS.

Dad wanted to know why.

Dad in my room on Wednesday Scout Night: Hey, Logan, why aren't you getting ready for Scouts? I could give you a ride.

Me: I'm not going.

Dad: Really? Why not?

Me: I don't want to.

I sort of yelled it.

Dad: Okay, okay. You don't have to.

Me: Good.

Dad: Is there anything you want to talk about?

Me: No.

Then all of a sudden Mom was at the door.

Mom: Hey, guys, what's the word?

Dad: Well, Logan here doesn't want to go to Scouts.

Mom: What? After that big man-making Klondike Derby campout?

If they only knew.

Me: Yeah. Even after that big man-making campout.

I said it slow and rude.

Mom: Is this about the lost sleeping bag, baby? It's okay.

Me: I know, Mom. You already said that, like, ten times.

Mom:

Dad:

Mom: Well, then let's go get shakes. The boys can take care of themselves.

Mom never offered to get shakes or ice cream or candy or anything like that. Never. And especially not without the other kids.

Me: Why?

Mom: Because your dad and I haven't had a lot of time to talk to you. Just the three of us.

It was something I knew I couldn't get out of. Their faces showed it.

Me: Fine.

So we went to Iceberg and got shakes.

I felt guilty they were taking me without the others, at first, but then I realized it made sense since everything was about me: Dr. Benson, me getting the best room, the playoff tickets, and now shakes.

In the middle of chocolate chip cookie dough, Mom said: Logan, what's going on?

I looked at her.

She was all sad again.

Dad: What your mother is trying to say, Logan, is that we love you and we want to help.

Me: Help with what? There's nothing wrong.

Mom: Come on, Logan. Give us a little credit.

Me: I'm fine.

Dad: At least tell us what happened on the campout. You haven't talked since you got home and Jack isn't answering his phone.

Me: It doesn't matter.

Mom: It does matter. It matters to us and it obviously matters to you.

Me: Uhhh.

Dad: Please?

Me:

Dad:

Mom:

Me:

Mom:

Me:

And then I told them.

I told them about the whole stupid campout.

Every single detail I could because it just came pouring out and I couldn't stop, but then I did stop when I felt like I was going to go too far. When I felt like I was almost going to tell them everything about even Zyler and Cami.

After that, when we got home,

My dad went straight to Jack and Patsy and Bruce's house.

In play practice we only had two weeks till the play.

Ms. March: Okay, people. Two weeks left.

Us:

Ms. March: You all need to step it up.

I was nervous because last practice I had to leave for a while to help Mr. Jeffries with something on the tree and they did the Lost Boy and pirate fight scene.

I hoped they didn't change where I was maybe going to be.

Ms. March: Let's start with "I Won't Grow Up."

I was in that one and everything was the same.

When we got to the fight part, Ms. March said: This scene is still problematic. We might have to restage some of you. Let's run straight through it and see what we can do.

Me:

And the worst part was right before the scene I saw Laurel in the back of the auditorium talking to Luke.

I don't think I'm going to get to be in front.

Mom said: Honey, a nice girl called to remind you about a project for Life Skills.

Me:

I had no idea.

Mom: She didn't leave her name but she said you were in charge of corn dogs and she wanted me to tell you word for word "Cigar? Toss it in a can. It is so tragic." Is that for health or something?

Me:

Laurel: Get down!

Me:

Laurel: You just don't get it. We are being watched. Very carefully.

Me: Whatever.

And then I thought this: What am I doing here? She never really talks to me except behind these bushes.

And I said this: I'm not going to meet you anymore.

Laurel: Why?

And her nose was so crooked.

Me: Because I don't want to.

Laurel: Why not?

Me:

And then I started to get up.

But she grabbed my hand.

She really grabbed it and yanked me down and kept holding my hand.

Laurel: Listen, Logan. If we're going to be friends you should probably tell me what happened at your old school and everything.

Me:

She was still holding my hand.

Me: Nothing happened.

Laurel: Come on.

Me: I can't.

Laurel: You can tell me. I promise I won't hate you or anything like that.

Me:

I sort of wanted to tell her. To be friends and everything and so she would know the truth.

Laurel: Please?

Me:

Her face – which was usually so loud and whatever she wanted and crooked nose and black pirate makeup – was different.

And I felt sad.

I said: I don't know.

Laurel:

Me:

Laurel:

Me:

Laurel:

Me: See, now you're not talking.

And she really wasn't. She was just sitting there – her head against the orange brick of the building. Her eyes closed.

I guess she didn't care if her hair got dirty.

Me: Laurel?

Laurel:

Me: Are you okay?

Laurel:

Me: Laurel?

I wasn't sure if she was breathing.

But then, finally, she opened her eyes.

Her: Please?

Me: Why do you want to know so bad?

Her: I don't know. Maybe because I think we should be friends.
I really want you to be my friend and I don't know if I can until
I know you're not what they say.

Me:

Dr. Benson says talking about it or going over it will make it
better.

He says I have to.

He doesn't know.

I said to him: No.

Dr. Benson: Logan, it's never going to be easy.

Me: I know that.

Dr. Benson: But if you can just get it out it will be a big relief.

Me:

Dr. Benson: Could you at least write it down?

Me:

Dr. Benson: Go somewhere alone and just write it out?

I don't think it will make me feel better.

But maybe.

*

To just write it all out, even the stuff I've never told anyone.

So many people wanted to know what happened.

Where he went after.

I have no idea, I'd say.

That's all.

But I knew.

This is what happened:

I saw Cami on Zyler's street, almost at his house.

It was after the whole family got to eat at Pete's Pancakes because of Mom's coupon and we passed her on the way home but

nobody noticed her but me.

Once we got home I said: Can I ride over to Zyler's real quick?

We were supposed to finish this one homework problem.

Mom: This late?

Me: It's only eight.

Mom sighed and then: Okay. But don't stay long.

And I didn't.

*

I didn't know I was actually going to go to Zyler's.

I just said that to get out of the house and see if Cami was still on Zyler's street and she probably didn't know it was his street, because how would she know?

Maybe she was just going on a walk and maybe I could talk to her or we could see if Zyler was home or something.

But when I got over there, I was just in time to see her go inside his door.

This is what I was: Mad.

Why was Cami at Zyler's?

Did they like each other?

Why didn't he tell me?

And maybe I almost went home, but then I had to see.

I dumped my bike in the side yard and went to try to look in his bedroom window.

No one there.

Lights on.

Zyler's dad would be mad.

I took a risk and climbed in.

Bump.

But there was music on.

In the front room.

I crawled out in the hall and felt sick.

Like last time, but this time I really was there.

I heard laughing.

And then talking.

Zyler's voice: Are you kidding me?

Girl's voice – Cami's obviously: Yeah. It was so funny.

Zyler's voice: How many times has he called you?

Cami: He never talks or anything. He just hangs up, but we have caller ID. Hello?

Zyler: Logan never thinks about stuff like that.

Cami: I could tell.

Laugh laugh laugh laugh laugh laugh laugh laugh laugh laugh laugh laugh laugh laugh

And never ever again.

Never ever again.

Ever.

I hate him.

I hate her.

I hate them.

I was slumped against the wall and almost about to leave

But then this:

Cami: Are you sure your dad's not going to come home?

She was sort of laughing.

Zyler: Nope. He's gone.

But I couldn't see anything.

And then there were these sounds.

It almost sounded like they were kissing.

I couldn't believe it.

Almost loud.

More kissing noises and I really couldn't believe it. Zyler never kissed girls. Neither of us did.

Cami: You're kind of good at this.

I wanted out of there. I was out of there. I couldn't believe it.

But then

But then, right then,

The worst sound.

At first I thought it was like a bunch of guys coming in because it was so loud and crashing things.

But then I realized it was just him and the sound of his voice, but he was raging.

And he was swearing and knocking things and heavy: Who the hell is this? What's going on?

And then there was this big crash – like a kick or something.

No music.

And Zyler's dad's system was worth like three thousand dollars or more. I moved down the hall closer to Zyler's room – just in case I had to run fast or something. I mean, if his dad looked down the hall and saw me.

Zyler: Dad – what's wrong with you?

There was something in his voice I couldn't say.

Zyler's dad: What's wrong with me? With *me*? I told you to never mess with my stuff. And who is *she*?

Zyler: I'm sorry, Dad. We just barely turned it on and she's just my friend. She's no one.

Zyler's dad: No one?

And then this:

A punching sound.

A crunch on the wall.

The sound of a body.

Girl sort of scream.

Zyler was gasping then when he said: Dad, please.

Zyler's dad: I swear I'm going to rip your guts out, you little?.?.?.

And then Cami's voice but it was really soft because I almost couldn't hear it and this: pleasenopleasenopleasenoplease

Heavy Breathing

A slap.

Zyler: Dad! Please.

Zyler's dad: Shut up, Zyler.

Zyler's voice but not his voice either: Dad. Dad. I'm sorry, okay? I'm really sorry. She's leaving. You're leaving, right, Cami?

Cami: Yes. Yes, I'm leaving.

And I think she might have been crying.

Zyler's dad: I said SHUT UP!

Another loud sound but more and Cami's high pitch and maybe

I should've run then and called the cops or got someone or done something 'cause then Cami was definitely crying.

Zyler's dad: Oh, I'm sorry, honey, did I make you upset?

Another slapping sound.

Cami: No. No. No, please. Stop.

I couldn't see her but I could hear her crying hard and saying no no no a lot and please please please.

Zyler's dad: Hey, Zy, she's my friend too.

Zyler: Stop it, Dad. Leave her alone, Dad.

Zyler's dad (and now his voice was all soft-like): I think I can make you feel better.

Cami: Please no. Don't.

And then there was a ripping sound and she screamed.

Zyler: Dad! What are you doing? Dad!! Get off her!

And then another crash and swearing and crashing and screaming and

Cami: STOP! STOP! STOP! STOP! STOP!

It kept going: her screaming, Zyler yelling, smashing, bodies, lamps.

Things were flying.

I can't do this I can't do this I can't do this.

In the hallway trapped I CAN'T DO THIS.

*

I CAN'T DO THIS.

But then it got worse because I couldn't see anything except maybe his dad slamming but then?.?.?.

I saw Cami.

She came in my view and she was crawling and her shirt was torn so that I could see her bra and everything and her face all red and the slamming by the TV and Zyler's groans.

She was moving so fast toward me, so fast, and I tried to get into Zyler's room before she saw me. I didn't want her to know I was there and that I was there the whole time. But then, just when I was almost all the way in his room, and I think maybe even she saw me and right then something happened.

A crack.

A crash.

A loud grunt.

Another crack.

A slump.

Then panting.

Cami: Oh my gosh. What'd you do?

Zyler:

Cami was whimpering and her voice was little.

I looked out and there was blood, so much blood, and one of Zyler's dad's trophies.

Zyler whispered: I think I killed my dad. I think I killed my dad.

And then louder: I think I just killed my dad.

*

That's when I ran.

I ran hard and loud and I didn't care and through his room and out the window and to my bike.

I just ran.

On my bike I thought this:

I just had to get away, get away.

But then I couldn't think anyway because what just happened? Zyler maybe killed his dad. And Cami's shirt was all ripped open and I didn't do anything. He maybe killed his dad. He's a murderer and he's not who I thought. I hate him I hate her I hate all of them. I'm so sorry. I'm so sorry.

But then: Zyler is my best friend.

But then: He killed his own dad.

But then: Zyler is my best friend.

When I got home

My mom: Logan? Is that you?

Me: Yeah.

Her: Did you get your homework done?

Me:

Because I had slammed my door.

But then, not thirteen minutes later and tapping on the window.

It was Zyler.

Zyler, with blood all over, standing in the window well.

*

I always run.

I always run, and maybe I am what they say.

I wrote this down and it's supposed to make me feel better.

It doesn't.

Zyler said through the window to meet him at the spot in five minutes.

He just said: Meet me at the spot in five minutes and don't tell anyone.

Me: Okay.

His face was all messed up and I could tell he was hurt pretty bad, but I didn't say anything.

After he left I didn't know what to do. He maybe killed his dad and what about Cami and they were kissing and then her shirt all open and torn and he might have killed his dad.

I thought.

I thought maybe I wouldn't go out there.

One minute.

Two minutes.

Three minutes.

Four minutes.

Five minutes.

At six minutes I started to walk around and around my room.

Seven minutes.

Eight minutes.

At nine minutes I sat on the floor and sort of just sat there.

Ten minutes.

And at eleven minutes was when I started to cry.

Twelve minutes.

Thirteen minutes.

At fourteen minutes Zyler was back at my window, and I wiped off my face to try to look normal even though I couldn't.

He looked at me and said: Open the window.

I didn't.

Zyler: Please, Logan. Open the window.

I still didn't.

Zyler: I'm out here with Cami and she's hurt and I don't know what to do. Please, Logan. I know you were there. I need you. Please help me.

I didn't.

And that's when Zyler, who was my best friend and so brave and so strong, that's when he started to cry too. Shaking. Crying.

And me shaking, crying.

Zyler: Please?

But I couldn't do anything.

I'm so sorry.

I'm so sorry.

I'm so sorry.

I want to die.

I want to die.

I'm so sorry.

*

I never saw Zyler again.

That night I heard the sirens and I didn't do anything.

I found out later that Zyler had taken Cami home and then I don't know where he went. But I do know that the cops found him and took him away because the next day I got up early and rode over there.

Police tape all around the house and then on the morning news: Sexual assault on a young girl. Possibly both a father and son involved in the attack. Details still being sorted out. Father in hospital in critical condition. Son in custody of the state. The 911 call put in by the father of the victim around midnight.

When they found out about it, Mom and Dad wanted to talk about it.

I said: I don't want to.

They said: Okay.

And okay.

*

After a few days, one of our teachers said that Zyler had moved and Cami transferred schools.

That was because everyone kept talking and wanting to know.

Macy said she was going to transfer schools too – next year.

I wanted to see what she knew so I asked her: What happened?

Her:

Me: I won't tell anyone. Is she okay?

Macy: No.

Me: What happened?

Macy: Don't act like you don't know, Logan. Everyone knows you were involved. You and Zyler. Everyone knows.

And then she stalked off and wouldn't ever talk to me except for when she had to, like, in school stuff.

I left my bike in our spot – just in case Zyler had run away from the cops or something and he came back or something and his bike wasn't there and he needed to get away.

Mom and Dad wanted to try to find him so I could call or contact him, but I didn't know how mad he'd be. I didn't know what I'd say.

Me: I don't feel like talking to him.

Them: Why?

Me: I just don't.

And then I'd go to my room.

*

Later, not long later, I didn't have to go to school.

Like Macy said, everyone knew and since I was Zyler's best friend it meant I was involved or I knew something or both.

I didn't want to go to school.

Mom and Dad said I didn't have to go.

It was okay.

So I stayed in my room and I didn't come out.

And then we moved.

I got an e-mail from Zyler sixteen days after he disappeared.

Email

Subject: Gone	Date: Today

From: Zyler

To: Logan

I don't know what to say to you. I still don't get it, Logan. You know I had to do it. I guess you made the decision you thought you had to make, but I never would have done that to you. I really don't think I would've.

Zy

I could never e-mail him back or anything.

I mean, I could because I did right then.

I pressed reply and put this:

Email

Subject: Re: Gone	Date: Today

From: Logan

To: Zyler

What happened? Where are You?

Log

He didn't write back.

I didn't try again.

Not really.

*

Dr. Benson: Haven't seen you in a while.

Me:

Dr. Benson: Nothing to say?

Me:

Dr. Benson: Come on, Logan. We're way past this.

Me:

Dr. Benson: What about Scouts? Anything to tell me there?

Me:

I had already told him about getting kicked in the balls and everything even though I didn't tell my dad for a while.

Dr. Benson: Are you going to the next activity?

Me: I don't know.

Dr. Benson: I know you can do it, Logan. You're tougher than those boys. I know you can do it.

Me:

Dr. Benson: Okay, how's the play?

Me: Okay.

Dr. Benson: Starts in a couple of weeks, right?

Me: Yeah.

Dr. Benson: Did you get the fight scene you were hoping for?

Me: Yeah.

Dr. Benson: Well, what about that assignment I gave you last time. How did that go?

Me:

Dr. Benson: Did you do it?

Me: Yeah.

Dr. Benson: You wrote everything down.

Me: Yes.

Dr. Benson: How did it go?

Me:

Dr. Benson:

Me:

Dr. Benson:

Me:

Dr. Benson: I see.

I sort of laughed.

Dr. Benson: Well, I have some good news for you.

I kept looking at my feet. He'd done this before and the good news was always something like: I'm proud of you and your parents are too.

But this time he said: I have Zyler's new e-mail address. It's changed now that he is with a permanent family.

I put Zyler's e-mail address on my mirror.

Dr. Benson said I could do anything I wanted with it.

He meant that it was okay if I didn't e-mail or anything.

I didn't know what I wanted.

*

One week until the play and I haven't been able to "rendezvous" with Laurel because she was sick and I wasn't.

But then when she wasn't sick anymore, I had to leave early for Mack and Ryan's club basketball games.

But then today

Ms. March: People! People!

But nobody cared because

Pirate costumes and too much makeup and who stole my sword and where's the flashlight for Tinkerbell and even more than that.

I was watching Ms. March and her tomato face get even more tomatoey.

Ms. March: PEOPLE!!!!!

And it was so loud that even the crew people stopped doing stuff.

Her hair was so big.

Ms. March in a very soft lots-of-heavy-breathing voice said: We don't have time. We don't have time for this.

It got louder and louder.

Ms. March: We don't have time for this!

Everyone stopped talking and we were sort of looking at each other because she was maybe going to blow.

Ms. March: We don't have time for this! We don't have time for this!

And right about there is when she fell.

Bam.

Fell.

Flat.

Still breathing but on the floor.

Nobody moved.

Not even anyone.

And then, after a really long time

Peter Pan: Uh, Ms. March?

Ms. March:

Peter Pan again: Ms. March?

Ms. March:

Peter Pan: Somebody call an ambulance!

And chaos again.

People screaming, girls surrounding Ms. March's up-and-down mass, boys running, set falling, and me just standing there.

Wondering.

What I should do.

I never know what to do.

So we all helped roll Ms. March over.

Including me.

She was alive still and someone thought maybe she was squishing herself and couldn't breathe as well on her stomach.

No one was in charge because the Peter Pan kid had taken off along with a bunch of other people yelling for help and ambulances.

The ones of us left all just stood there looking at her.

I knew she should probably have her head propped up.

And we should probably talk to her.

Or see if she could talk.

I mean, you could tell she was breathing – the big mask necklace she wore was slowly moving up and down.

But everyone just stood there.

So

I

Knelt

Down

And

Put

Her

Head

In

My

Lap.

Everyone stepped closer.

Me: Ms. March, can you hear me?

Her:

Me, and I said it a little louder this time: Ms. March, can you hear me?

She moaned a bit and there was so much sweat dripping off her face. I tried to wipe it off with my sleeve.

Me: Ms. March?

Her: a louder moan.

Everyone stepped back and she sort of rolled a bit. But not over, just around or something.

I wiped more sweat off and I didn't know what to do next.

What do I do next?

And I thought I should probably keep talking or get her to talk or respond or probably, probably sing.

That's what Mom did for me when I was sick.

But Ms. March wasn't sick.

She was almost dead or something.

But

Then what?

So I almost did it. I started to almost sing the song that got me the part: "Where Can I Turn for Peace?" I even said "Where?.?.?."

But then three ambulance guys were there and loud and move back and hang on, kid, let us take over and she's all right. She's going to be fine. Why don't you kids go home for now. It looks like she's just in shock a bit. A faint. Go home.

I sat there and watched from far away sort of.

And she was fine.

She sat up.

She said: Oh my!

They said: You're going to be fine.

She said: No, I'm not. I've got a play to put on.

And that's when I really did go home.

*

Since I've been seeing Dr. Benson things are sort of better.

Like yesterday I almost helped Mack with his math.

Mom was out shopping, Dad was at work, Ryan and I were on the couch watching TV, and Mack was behind us at the kitchen table.

Mack: I hate math.

Ryan: Shut up, Mack. I can't hear.

Me:

And then we kept watching.

Mack: I hate it. I hate it. I hate it.

Mack was so uptight about everything.

He kept erasing and erasing and moaning and making noises.

Then he yelled: I HATE IT!

Ryan said: Holy crap, man. If you don't shut your mouth I'm going to shut it for you. We're trying to watch TV.

I looked back at him and I knew he was going to freak out.

Mack: Why don't you shut it? You shut it.

A pencil whizzed past our heads.

Ryan started to laugh.

Mack: Oh, you think that's funny?

He threw his math book hard at Ryan. Ryan ducked and laughed again.

Mack was furious but instead of attacking Ryan like he normally would he just took off upstairs.

Ryan: Wuss.

Me:

But I did sort of laugh.

Normally, I mean, since Zyler, I wouldn't have done anything after that.

I would have just sat there.

Or more likely I would have been in my room instead of up with the twins.

But instead I went upstairs.

And instead I got all Mack's stuff together and went and knocked on his door.

I did it even though Ryan said: Don't do anything. He's an idiot.

I knocked and then I said: Do you want me to help you?

His door:

Me:

His door:

Me: Come on.

His door: Go away.

Me: Are you sure?

His door:

Me: Okay.

I left all his stuff by his door for when he needed it.

I decided I wasn't going to meet Laurel anymore because I didn't want to tell her everything but then she said this: I'm not scared of you because I know it's not true.

Me:

Laurel: Aren't you going to say something?

Me: Ummm.

Laurel: Come on, Logan.

But I didn't know what to say.

Laurel: Don't you want to know why?

Her upper lip twitched and she pulled off a scab from her elbow.

Me: Okay. Why?

Laurel: Bruce has been telling everyone that you and another guy -assaulted this girl at your last school and that you are a sicko that will wind up a stalker or even worse.

She took a breath.

I didn't.

Laurel: Bruce said he knew because his mom talked to your mom and then she did some calling around to find out what really happened. Bruce's mom thinks she knows everyone and everything. You should have been here last year when they fired the bus driver for absolutely no reason, but mainly because of stuff Bruce's mom claimed to know.

She took another breath.

I still didn't.

Laurel: But see, I know what Bruce said about you isn't true because I asked my mom if she knew anything about you or your last school because she's on the school board. Remember?

Me:

Laurel: Well, she told me the whole story so you don't have to worry.

And then she was still picking at another scab but she was looking right at me.

Me:

Laurel: Well? Is it true?

Me: What?

Laurel: What my mom said.

Me: How do I know what your mom said?

Laurel: Oh, well, she totally knew about an incident with kids at your school and she told me the whole story about how a girl did get abused – almost raped, even – and it was at this drug house and the kid and his dad did it and she knows that both the kid and the dad are locked up. They talked about it while they were discussing the D.A.R.E. proposal. Mom said that everyone involved was on drugs. So then I asked her about why you would have anything to do with it.

Breath.

Me:

Laurel: And my mom didn't know about you specifically, but she said she heard that the kid's friend may have seen the whole thing happen or something. Was that you?

Me:

Laurel: So?

I just looked at her.

Laurel: So?

Me:

Laurel: Is it true? Is that what happened?

Me:

Laurel: Come on, Logan. I know you didn't do it.

Me:

Laurel: And I knew all along that you weren't a molester or abuser or whatever.

Me:

Laurel: So you didn't really have anything to do with it, did you? Right?

Me:

Laurel: Just say you didn't do it and I'll know it's true. You didn't do it.

Screw it.

Me: Actually, I kind of did do it.

I don't think Laurel knew what to do after that because she just stared at me and I stared back.

We kept staring.

Stare

Stare

Stare

And then I told her.

I told her about Zyler and how he wasn't drugged up and how he tried to stop his dad.

I mean, how he did stop his dad.

And how he was my best friend.

160

Ever.

Even if he wasn't what I thought sometimes and I think maybe he was mad at me, but maybe it was okay.

And I told her how I didn't actually do it but sort of: I knew and I was there and I didn't do anything. I never do anything, almost never.

Laurel:

Me:

Laurel: So you actually saw her with her shirt all ripped up?

Me: I guess.

She looked at me and then leaned her head against the brick again – her eyes closed. I knew then that she'd never want to be my friend. No one would. It was my fault. It was my fault. I was crapstock.

Her eyes still closed, she said: But sad Eva saved a stub.

Me: What?

Laurel: Duh.

And then I said: Oh.

Laurel: Who's doing your makeup for the play?

Me: I don't know.

Laurel: Okay, I'm doing it. Stacy Beck is trying to say she's the makeup person, but she's so bad at it. You should have seen the play we did last year for sixth grade graduation. She made all the colonial women look like hookers. Mrs. Porter almost had a cow because she had no idea how awful Stacy was going to be because Stacy was saying she was so good because she lives in a mortuary and sometimes helps with the makeup; she told Mrs. Porter that she had a ton of experience. You should have seen Mrs. Porter's face when we came out. We still had to do the whole thing like that anyway. Did you guys do a play at your old school?

Me:

And that was it.

I might meet her at the mall for corn dogs this Saturday.

The night before the play I went to Scouts.

I had promised Dr. Benson.

I could do it.

At Scouts nobody talked to me as usual.

We were making canteens out of gourds and mine was really good.

I was carving out the inside when this: One more word out of you and I'm not going to hold back.

It was Jack.

And Bruce.

Bruce: Dad, I just don't get how to do it.

Jack: I explained it. I showed you all. I even started yours and I'm sick of your whining attitude. Now shut up and carve your gourd.

Bruce: But?.?.?.

Jack: Shut up!

Bruce was turning red and didn't say anything.

None of us were saying anything and even though I didn't want to, I sort of felt bad for Bruce.

Five minutes later he said quietly: Dad?

Jack:

Bruce: Dad?

Jack: Bruce, I am warning you.

Bruce: I just have one question.

That's when Jack hit him.

He hit him hard.

Bruce was on the floor.

We all just sat there.

Sat

Sat

Sat

And Bruce was huddled and sort of crying and Jack was yelling: I told you to shut up. I told you to SHUT UP!

Bruce: But, Dad?.?.?.

Jack: SHUT UP!

And he raised his fist again.

That's when I yelled as loud as I could.

Everyone looked at me.

Even Bruce.

Me: Leave him alone. LEAVE HIM ALONE!

Silent.

Silent.

And then I left.

The next night: *Peter Pan* opening night.

They were all yelling and screaming so loud.

I didn't know what to do – how to act or anything – so I just stood on the side of the tree and bowed a bunch of times.

Then tomorrow is the last day of school.

Most of my makeup was on my sleeve because Laurel had put so much on.

She said: You have to have a lot – you're under the lights.

I guess she was right.

There were a lot of lights.

And the best part was the fight scene because even though I was nervous,

I was sweating and sweating and sweating some more,

we did it just like we practiced, but even the spin move was better than I thought it would be.

And so they were still yelling and even standing up: Mom with her huge stomach, Dad, Mack, Ryan, Dr. Benson (I didn't really believe he would come) all standing up and yelling and clapping.

Ms. March said it was the best fight scene she'd ever seen in a school play.

Laurel gave me a book called *Palindromes?—The Best of the Best* and whispered: You were great.

Next year we're doing the *Pirates of Penzance* because of all the pirate costumes.

I might be the Pirate King.

*

That night.

Email

Subject: Hey   **Date: Today**

From: Logan

To: Zyler

Hey Zy,

We moved. To Judge. Over by the mall. And I'm a
Lost Boy in the play Peter Pan. It's pretty cool. I also
have this friend who's a girl named Laurel but she
might change her name to Laral because she's into
palindromes. Like when the words go frontwards and
backwards. I kind of like them too. Here's one: A
Santa at NASA.

Logan.

P.S. Maybe we could talk on the phone sometime
unles you don't want to.

P.P.S. I left my bike for you.